LANGUAGE OF LOVE

In Geneva, Henry and I visited a small clothing shop. I picked out a multicolored shawl, and asked in French how much it cost. I was relieved that the shopkeeper answered me in French, since I knew Henry would jump at the chance to correct me. As I was paying, a woman entered the store, looking very worried.

"Excuse me, have you seen my wallet?" she asked the shopkeeper in English. The shopkeeper looked at her, not understanding. I explained in French that the woman had lost her wallet, and managed to translate her description of it.

"Ah, *merci.*" The shopkeeper clasped my hands in relief.

Henry grinned at me. "You were great."

"Thanks, but I could have used your help."

He shrugged. "You didn't need me. For once, I thought I should stay out of your way."

I didn't know what to say. It seemed as though, for the first time, he understood me. The thought sent trickles of warmth through me. As we walked, Henry's hand brushed against mine, and I wondered what it would be like to have his arms around me. *For crying out loud,* I told myself, *you're not even supposed to like Henry.*

Language Of Love

Rosemary Vernon

BANTAM BOOKS
TORONTO • NEW YORK • LONDON • SYDNEY • AUCKLAND

RL 6, IL age 11 and up

LANGUAGE OF LOVE
A Bantam Book / December 1984
Reprinted 1985

Cover photo by Pat Hill

ISBN 0-553-24357-8

Published simultaneously in the United States and Canada

Printed and bound in Great Britain by Hunt Barnard Printing Ltd.

O   0 9 8 7 6 5 4 3 2 1

For Eve Becker,
who knows the story better than I
and who has muddled through it with me.

Special thanks to John Foster, French instructor and adviser for the foreign exchange program at Emma Willard School, Troy, New York, and to Emma Willard's 1983 exchange students for sharing their delightful travel experiences.

Chapter One

It was just one of those days. I couldn't wait to get to school and hear the news, but the day didn't go quite the way I had planned it.

The morning started off smoothly enough. Both Mom and Dad were off to work before I even made it downstairs for breakfast. My genius brother, Tim, left the house shortly after to get an early start on an important research paper—he goes to college in a nearby town. But just as I was sitting down to eat my soft-boiled egg and toast, a scream shattered the peaceful morning.

I went outside to investigate the sound and found Mrs. DeLaurio, the sweet old lady who lives next door, lying in her garden. She'd fallen down and hurt her hip. Well, I helped her up and settled her in her own living room, but I knew she should see a doctor. After thinking about it for a minute, I ran back to our house, got the keys to Mom's old car, and then dashed back to Mrs. DeLaurio's house. I drove her to the hospital, but by the time she was checked in and x-rayed, it was almost two o'clock, too late to go to school.

And that's why I was back in the car at three, creeping down the traffic-clogged streets, trying to make it to Smiley's Soda Shop before Lacey and Ellen left. They are my two best friends, and they'd be able to tell me the news I'd been dying to hear all day long. "I hope I made it," I whispered.

There had been twenty applicants for the Windsor High-Swiss Exchange Program, but only six would be selected. Six out of twenty wasn't bad odds, and since I was a good student, I had an even better chance. I'd had a lot of French, too—I was in my third year. But then again, seniors were chosen first, and I was still a junior. I tried not to frown. I had to be chosen, I just had to. Three weeks with a Swiss family was something I definitely didn't want to miss.

I found a spot in the parking lot outside Smiley's and hurried toward the door. Through the plate glass window I glimpsed Lacey and Ellen and broke into a run.

"Hey, Robin." A hand grabbed me. I whirled

around to see Henry Bouchet's smirking face. Great, just the person I wanted to see right then, the most conceited guy in my French class.

"I'm sort of late, Henry," I growled.

"I just wanted to say congratulations, Robin."

I stared at him, knowing right away what he was talking about. But I hadn't expected such good news from someone I disliked so much. "I'm going to Switzerland?" I said quietly, rooted to the sidewalk.

"Yes, but that's not the best part. I'm going, too."

I shot Henry a look. He was smiling in that annoying way of his, and I just knew he was laughing at me. I studied his long, narrow face and nose. His dark green eyes were staring at me from under a lock of his wavy, blondish-brown hair. He was disturbingly good-looking. "I didn't think you'd been at Windsor long enough to qualify for the exchange program."

"The rules were changed this year. You only have to have been at Windsor two months to apply," he said. "Good thing I transferred from my last school three months ago." He smiled smugly. "So, aren't you going to congratulate me?"

"Sure. Congratulations," I mumbled.

"I was surprised you weren't in school today,"

he remarked. "I couldn't imagine why you'd miss assembly, today of all days."

"I didn't plan to, but an emergency came up." Why was I explaining myself to Henry of all people, the guy who always put me down?

Ever since Henry had transferred to Windsor, he'd been a thorn in my side. I knew I shouldn't let it get to me, but the idea that conceited Henry Bouchet with his maddening command of French could charm his way into our upper-level French class really burned me. He sure hadn't sweated it out in Mr. List's class for more than two years the way the rest of us had. I was the best student until Henry came. But within two weeks of his arrival, he'd grabbed the student teaching position I'd had my heart set on—helping in the beginning French class. It's true that Mr. List had never promised me the job, but I figured he'd pick me because I was the only A student in third year—before Henry's arrival, that is.

Needless to say, I'd been proud of the fact that I had a certain status in the French department, but when Henry came he didn't only take my job but he also dragged me down a couple of notches in the teacher's eyes.

And, can you believe it, when Henry was offered the teaching position, he came to me with the "good" news. "Aren't you excited for me, Robin?" he'd asked.

"Extremely. Congratulations." Inside, I was burning with envy. Did he have to rub it in? Did he have to brag?

I still remember every detail of the scene. I was thinking how attractive Henry was and that I wished he weren't. "I've wanted a chance to put my French to work for a long time," he said. "I'm surprised I was given the job since I just came to Windsor."

"So am I." *You just push people out of the way and get exactly what you want, huh, Henry?* I thought to myself.

"Didn't you want me to do this?" he asked me, studying me closely.

"I don't care." His scrutiny made my skin prickle, and I averted my eyes so he couldn't read my true feelings.

"Then you're not serious about French?"

"Oh, not at all," I shot back. The truth is, nobody takes three years of French unless they're very serious about it. In fact, I dreamed of working at the United Nations as a translator someday, but I didn't tell Henry that.

Then Henry invited me to go and celebrate with him, but I said no because I had to go to work. The thought crossed my mind that maybe he was disappointed. He didn't have very many friends at school back then since he'd moved so recently.

"Robin?"

Henry's voice beside me pulled me back to the present.

"Oh, I guess I was daydreaming about the trip," I said, blushing.

"Just think," he said slyly, "we'll be together for three weeks in Switzerland."

"How sweet." I grimaced, wishing he didn't have to be so obnoxious all the time. "Who else is going?" I asked.

"Melissa Burns, Tracy Simmons, John Wycombe, and Dennis Winter," he said. "You and I'll be the only juniors, but we'll be in good company."

"Hey, Robin." Thank goodness, Lacey to the rescue. She must have spotted us standing outside and guessed that I was having a hard time getting away from Henry. She ran toward us quickly. "He told you you were accepted, right?" I nodded, grinning. "Congrats." She gave me a big bear hug.

Ellen came up behind her, then slid her arms around me. "Good for you, Robin. I'm so excited for both of you." She tugged me toward the door of the soda shop.

"Of course Robin's going. I told Mr. List I needed a research assistant, and she'd be just the one," Henry said, grinning like an idiot. He was referring to my job at the public library. I worked at the information center, so I was always helping people find research materials. It was a good job. I learned a lot there and was always finding out interesting bits of information. Also, the money I made would help finance the trip to Switzerland. I didn't understand why Henry had to make fun of the job.

But then, Henry was one of those types who has to upstage everybody else. Sure, he was smart, but he had to brag about it. His usual pattern was to start by pretending to be concerned about something or offering advice and then to suddenly begin bragging about a grade or some great accomplishment. What a pain!

Lacey turned to me, again drawing attention away from Henry—bless her heart. "By the way, Robin, where have you been all day?" she asked. "We've been calling your house constantly. This was one day nobody expected you to skip classes."

"Actually, I was in the hospital," I said teasingly. Then I calmed everybody by quickly explaining what had happened to Mrs. DeLaurio as I pushed open the door to Smiley's.

We three girls slid into a booth. Henry saw some friends near the counter and joined them. "See you, Robin. It's nice to hear what a good

Samaritan you can be," he said, sarcastically referring to the help I'd given Mrs. DeLaurio.

"Ha-ha, Henry." I breathed a sigh of relief to see him go.

"He's cute," commented Ellen.

"He's a real pain," I grumbled. "I just hope we don't have to see too much of each other on this trip. At least we'll be living with different Swiss families."

"Oh, don't worry. You'll see so many new things, you'll be too busy to let Henry bother you," Lacey said practically.

"Yeah, you're right." Suddenly excitement overcame me as I realized I was actually going to go abroad. "It's going to be a terrific three weeks in Switzerland. Nothing's going to spoil a trip like this for me."

"Well, I'm looking forward to the three weeks when the Swiss kids will be here!" Ellen said excitedly. "I can't wait."

"Hey, I'll be back in a second," Lacey broke in all of a sudden as she rose from the table.

"Oops, must be Michael Moore," Ellen whispered.

Lacey had been in love with Michael for ages, and now that the feeling was mutual, she was ecstatic. I was happy for Lacey, but she sure acted silly whenever Michael was around. I didn't really understand. You see, I'd never been in love before. Sure, I'd dated, but I'd never experienced that crazy, wild feeling I'd read about in books.

I saw Melissa Burns and Tracy Simmons on the other side of Smiley's, and I waved. They came over to talk about the trip and sat down in our booth. "Henry told you, right?" Melissa guessed.

"Yes." I rolled my eyes.

"He's not so bad, Robin. You don't have to make a face every time his name is mentioned," Ellen said.

"He just likes to give you a hard time," Tracy added reflectively.

"Well, the school better charter a jumbo jet for this trip, just to accommodate Henry's head," I said.

Melissa and Tracy laughed, but I could see Ellen shaking her head.

Chapter Two

Just before dinner that day, I was busy shoveling a light coating of snow from the front walk. Every once in a while I threw a snowball up at my brother's window. He was in his bedroom on the second floor, his bent head silhouetted behind the curtain, busy with homework. He and I took turns doing the shoveling, but quite often when it was his turn, he'd pay me to do it so that he could study, which was fine with me. I needed the money, and he needed the time.

I finished the shoveling, stamped the snow off my boots, and entered the house noisily. Then I put on a Willie Nelson album and started to help fix dinner.

"I've been looking through the catalogs for clothes for your trip, Robin," my mom said. She was wearing one of her favorite caftans. Mom and I look alike, with the same brown eyes, arched eyebrows, slightly upturned noses, and heads of curly, dark brown hair. "We'll have to take a trip to the mall and pick up some light shirts and a dress or two," she said. Trust Mom to be thinking months in advance about a wardrobe.

My mom is the clothes authority; Dad is our real estate expert; and my brother Tim is our resident scientist.

"It's pretty hard to imagine spring clothes when we just got into sweaters, Mom," I reminded her.

"It's never too early to plan," she insisted.

"All right, Mom," I said. "I'll try to find the time."

"Great, honey. Now can you give me a hand finishing the salad?"

My father breezed in the door a few minutes later and wrapped me in an affectionate hug. "It's great to have a traveler in the family," he said, beaming. "Your mother phoned me while you were out shoveling to tell me the wonderful news. Just think, if we ever take that family vacation in France we've been talking about, you can be our interpreter."

"There'll be a small charge for services rendered," I said, teasing him.

Dad tugged playfully at my hair. "Will a plane ticket cover your fee?" he quipped, and we all laughed.

Our French teacher, Mr. List, is tall and lanky, with curly hair and a thin mustache. He arrived at our first exchange-program meeting, looking smart in a blue suit and a navy tie.

Melissa Burns nudged me from behind. She'd had a huge crush on Mr. List at the beginning of the school year and used to stare at his yearbook photo every day. The whole infatuation sort of fizzled after he married a violinist in the city orchestra and Mel realized her love was doomed forever. But she still thought he was awfully cute.

"Doesn't he look great today?" she hissed in my ear.

"Terrific," I agreed.

"I'm really psyched that he's going to chaperon us in Switzerland," she said.

"I'll bet you are. Are you sure you've completely recovered from that crush you had on him?" I asked. "It would be a terrible waste for you to go around Switzerland daydreaming about a hopeless case."

"Mmm. It's only when he speaks French that I go wild."

"Hey, Robin, here comes your heartthrob,"

Melissa said with a sly grin. I looked up to find Henry striding toward us. I turned so he couldn't see and made a face at Melissa.

"*Bonjour*, Robin," he said, sitting down at the desk across from me.

"Hi, Henry."

"You dropped this in the hallway." He slapped my French-English dictionary on my desk top. "I knew you'd go crazy without it, especially since we're playing store today." Mr. List used role playing to teach us how to handle situations we'd be facing in Switzerland, such as going into a restaurant or shop. "I wouldn't want to see you speechless," Henry said, pointing out, that he knew I was better at writing French than at speaking it—especially in front of the entire class.

"Thanks for the book," I told him stiffly.

"You're welcome." He looked very smug. Lately Henry had been more cocky than ever and seemed to delight in picking on me.

In an attempt to get the meeting underway, Mr. List looked pointedly at Henry, cleared his throat, and began to speak. "We'll be meeting here once a week until our departure. I'm going to teach you about Swiss currency and the metric system and show you slides taken by last year's exchange students. We'll also do a lot more role playing."

Mr. List began to pace back and forth in front of us, using the blackboard pointer as a walking stick. I heard Melissa giggle behind me. "We'll be visiting the southwestern and western parts of Switzerland. You know, of course, that it's the French-speaking area. We certainly wouldn't want to send our French students to the German- or Italian-speaking provinces," he joked. "The Canton of Neuchâtel, where you'll be, uses a purer form of French than the rest of Switzerland, and that is one of the reasons we chose it. Also, it is relatively close to Geneva and Bern, cities where you will be able to see very old architecture and ruins as well as modern developments.

"First, we'll fly to Zurich and then change planes for Bern. We'll spend a few days there sightseeing and getting accustomed to the culture. Then we'll go on to the city of Neuchâtel, where you'll join your host families and attend the host school, the Lycée Vinol."

"I wonder if I'll have to bring a converter for my blow dryer," Melissa whispered in my ear.

"In a couple of weeks," Mr. List continued, "we will learn who our host families are, and we can then correspond with them. That way we can get to know them through letters and photos before we actually meet. You'll go to classes for the morning hours with your Swiss 'brothers' and 'sisters.' "

"Maybe my brother will be a hunk!" Melissa hissed, causing me to giggle out loud.

"In the afternoons," Mr. List went on, frowning at Mel and me, "we'll take trips together to museums and other attractions. After that, you'll have free time to sightsee—but always go with someone.

"You're going to experience some difficulties with language, so expect them. Don't be afraid to use your French. No one will expect you to speak like a native. Your host family won't make fun of you or like you less because of your accent. Remember, they want you there just as much as you want to be there. I'll be around, too, to help you with any problems."

I began to realize that we were embarking on a huge adventure, even bigger than I'd imagined.

Tracy Simmons shot me a wide-eyed look. She raised her hand timidly. "Is anyone in our host family going to speak English?" she asked.

"Don't worry, Tracy. Since your Swiss 'brothers' and 'sisters' will be coming to America for their own three-week adventures, they'll have to know some English. They'll be able to meet you halfway."

The group breathed a collective sigh of relief, except for Henry, who seemed totally unaffected by and calm about everything Mr. List had told us. I could just see the rest of us standing out like dumb tourists in Switzerland while he blended in perfectly and made us look like idiots.

"Is the city of Neuchâtel large?" Melissa asked.

"No, it's a fairly small community on Lake of Neuchâtel, and it's surrounded by vineyards." Mr. List passed around some snapshots from the previous year's trip. Then we did a little role playing before the meeting broke up.

"What do you know about this part of Switzerland?" Henry quizzed me as I bundled into my winter coat at my locker.

"Is this the sixty-four-thousand-dollar question?" I responded defensively.

He laughed. "You don't have to answer if you don't have anything to say."

That was almost like a challenge, and so I rattled off a few facts as we walked toward the door. "I know that Neuchâtel has a population of approximately thirty-five thousand and that it's below the Jura Mountains. During the eighteenth century it became a commercial and industrial hub for watchmaking and fabric printing," I quoted from my European history book. Whew, sometimes all those hours in the library really paid off.

"Very good." Henry patted the top of my head condescendingly, but I thought I detected a glint of admiration in his eyes. Secretly that pleased me. Henry opened the front door, and I stole a glance at him. The late-afternoon sunlight illuminated his hair, and it shone so beautifully I almost wanted to reach out and touch it.

"After you," he said, holding the door open. "Beauty before brains."

Immediately I bristled. He'd finally come out and said it. He thought he was smarter than me.

I rolled my eyes and gave him a little push through the doorway. "A person could grow very tired of you, Henry," I said angrily. "By the way, how'd you do on the French test last week?"

"Oh, fabulously, of course."

"Doesn't your ego ever deflate?" I wondered aloud.

"Not often. How'd you do?"

"Great, thank you." I thrust my nose in the air and strode ahead of him, but I could hear Henry laughing behind me.

"A person could get tired of *me*! Look who's talking."

Chapter Three

After three months of waiting, March finally arrived. The weekend before our departure for Europe, Ellen threw us a bon voyage party that could be heard blocks away. The mailbox in front of Ellen's driveway was lit by a flashing yellow bulb that John Wycombe, one of the exchange students, had pried off a construction sawhorse. He'd presented it to Ellen "so that guests can find the house."

"John's going to be a lot of fun in Switzerland if he keeps pulling tricks like this," Lacey said as we trudged toward the front door.

"He'll be just fine, as long as he doesn't bring his box of disguises," I told her. "Remember the time he dressed in the bird costume and skipped down Main Street?"

"That was on a dare, Robin," Lacey reminded me. "Just don't challenge him to do anything once you're abroad."

Wouldn't you know it, when Lacey rang the doorbell, John answered it, wearing those glasses with eyeballs attached to springs. Well, that sent us into hysterics.

"Sorry about him," Ellen said, ushering us inside. "He was going to wear his Incredible Hulk costume, but I thought that would be a bit too much."

A group of kids started talking to John and me about the trip.

"I'll send you all a postcard," I promised.

"Oh, Robin, if I lose a few pounds, do you think you could squeeze me in your suitcase?" Lacey begged. We laughed and made our way over to the snack table.

A little later on I saw Lacey and Michael Moore dancing to a slow song, and I noticed Ellen talking intently with Bruce Litton. Suddenly I felt alone. Seeing all those people warm and cozy together made me feel a little jealous. Just because I hadn't ever had a real boyfriend didn't mean I liked being on my own all the time.

"Want to dance?"

I turned to find Henry, of all people, looking at me expectantly.

"Did you just ask me to dance?" I asked in disbelief.

"Yeah, but if you don't answer quickly, I'm likely to take back the question." He cocked his head to one side. "Shall I ask in French?"

"English is just fine," I said, surprised as Henry took me in his arms.

"A guy's got to be brave to ask you to dance, with the way you react."

"You'd better be careful," I shot back. "I might be even more dangerous on the dance floor." I laughed and pretended to step on his toes.

The dance was slow and sweet. I braced myself, expecting Henry to do or say something embarrassing, as was his usual style. But he glided me across the floor smoothly, in a manner that left me totally breathless.

"You're a good dancer," he said.

I surveyed him carefully, but there was no sign of his usual smirk. "Thank you," I responded tentatively.

His arm tightened around my waist, and he started humming the tune we were dancing to in my ear, his breath fluttering against my hair. A pleasant thrill ran along my skin—I couldn't believe that I was actually enjoying dancing with Henry Bouchet.

"Um, Henry," I muttered, embarrassed by his closeness, "tell me about your Swiss hosts."

"Their name is Sardeau. Elise is the daughter, and she sounds nice. She's written me twice and says she's very interested in music. She has a record collection of traditional Swiss music that sounds really neat."

"Mine are the Aubers," I said. "Dominique, the daughter, is interested in fashion. She can't wait to see what we Americans are wearing. She wrote me that she'd like to see a baseball game when she comes over here."

"I have a great-uncle who supposedly lives in the Neuchâtel area, and I'm going to try to find him," Henry said.

"Really? That's exciting. Do you think you'll be able to track him down?"

"I don't know, but I might not get another chance for years."

Gradually Ellen had been turning the lights down as the music got more and more romantic. By now they were so dim that at first I didn't recognize Ann Tolbert when she tapped Henry on the shoulder.

"Henry, didn't you promise me a dance?"

He looked a little stunned. "Oh, sure, Ann. Next one, OK?"

Ann nodded but didn't leave us. "Are you excited about Switzerland?" *The ultimately dumb question*, I thought to myself. *Wouldn't anyone be excited?*

21

"Yeah, very," Henry answered, sounding a little annoyed. "Did you know Robin's going, too?"

Ann's gaze passed over me in a quick appraisal. Henry's eyes lingered on mine, and I thought he was going to make a smart remark. I smiled sweetly, as if my smile could deflect what he might say.

"No, I didn't know," Ann said.

"Well," Henry said slowly, grinning at me, "that's probably because we've decided to ship her in the baggage compartment."

"Henry!" I exclaimed, watching him move onto the dance floor with Ann.

"Do you want to dance, Robin?"

It was John, complete with the silly eyeball glasses.

"Can you take the glasses off?" I asked.

"No," he said with utmost seriousness. "They're part of my new identity."

"Well, I hope this identity is not coming with us to Switzerland," I teased. Other dancers were giggling at us as John's "eyeballs" jiggled around in front of my face.

"Hey, John, do you plan on making a public nuisance of yourself in Europe?" Melissa cried.

"He's going to embarrass me half to death right now!" I told her when he didn't answer.

John's dancing left much to be desired, and his funny glasses kept knocking me in the head.

As he clumsily turned me around, I caught Henry staring at us from across the room. The lights were dim, outlining his face in shadow. He looked as handsome as the Swiss boys we'd seen in slides.

I averted my gaze, not sure if he was looking at me or at John's silly disguise. Trust me to accept a dance with the party clown.

Abruptly the music stopped in midsong. Ellen came forward. "Presents for the travelers," she said happily, presenting each of us with a gift wrapped in gold foil.

Tracy peeled the paper off hers as if she were peeling an orange. Dennis Winter, a short, owlish-looking boy, tugged at the elastic golden thread on his package, waiting for the others to open theirs. Henry ripped his open quickly and lifted a digital mini-clock out of the folded tissue.

"Hey, these are great!" Melissa exclaimed, holding her clock up for all to see.

"Everyone got the same thing, no arguments," Ellen said.

"Chosen so you won't miss a minute of fun in Switzerland," Lacey added.

There was a chorus of "thank yous" from the exchange students.

"Who knows?" Celia Thorne piped up. "My sister fell in love while hiking in the Swiss Alps last year. It could happen to any of you, then you won't care what time it is!"

Everyone cracked up. Henry strolled around setting everyone's clocks.

"Let me see your clock." Henry held his palm out, and I gave it to him. He fiddled with it, then returned it to me. "There, now you have the proper time—that is, if you care what time it is," he added. I wondered if he was referring to what Celia had said about her sister.

I turned beet red. "Oh, thank you. Maybe you can help fix cuckoo clocks while we're in Switzerland," I suggested. *What a stupid thing to say!* I thought, suddenly self-conscious. Henry smiled and laughed at my dumb joke, anyway.

"To the travelers!" Ellen made a toast with her soda. Henry, the four other exchange students, and I were suddenly surrounded by well-wishers who were clinking plastic cups of soft drinks.

In the excitement Henry pushed against me. The scent of his cologne and his nearness filled me with a heady sensation. I would've moved away instantly if I didn't realize it would have looked funny to bolt suddenly from the crowd. So I was relieved when a good record came on and the group broke up.

Ellen and Bruce and Lacey and Michael joined the mass of dancing partners. I started to feel a little lonely again, watching people pair up, so I took my ginger ale to the back porch and gazed out over the tops of trees to the mountains, black against the violet-blue sky. I could hear a couple talking in hushed tones.

So, Celia's sister had fallen in love in Switzerland. I wondered if that could happen to me. Sometimes I thought "falling in love" only happened in books, although many of my friends assured me it was for real.

Of course, I wasn't going to Switzerland in the hopes of falling in love. That hadn't entered my mind until that night. But now I realized that Switzerland would be twice as romantic as being at home. Who knew *what* could happen? This trip might turn out to be a dream come true.

Chapter Four

This is it, I thought to myself. *I'm finally on my way to Switzerland!* The ride to New York's Kennedy Airport had been a long one, and my body ached from not moving. *Great, now all I've got is another seven hours on airplanes,* I thought. I glanced at my watch and suddenly felt alarmed. "Come on! We've got to hurry. That accident on the road really made us late. You don't want me to miss my plane, do you?" I yelled at my family.

And when we finally found the terminal, I learned, to my horror, that my flight was already boarding. I was told to carry my own suitcase on board since it was too late to be loaded.

"Tim, grab my suitcase, please!"

"Robin, hurry!" Mom cried. The four of us started running toward the boarding area.

"Passengers only," said a man in a uniform, stopping us at a contraption that blocked the hallway. "Put your suitcase up here for x-raying and walk slowly through that metal detector."

"We'll be late!" I said to the official. As if I weren't worried enough, the metal detector let out a loud shriek as I stepped through. Everyone stared at me. I felt as if some CIA agent was about to come and take me away as a spy.

"What's wrong?" I asked, scared to death.

"Take off your jewelry and anything metal you're carrying and walk through again," the official told me.

I took off my heavy necklace, a going-away present from Lacey, and my earrings and emptied my pockets of some change. When I walked through again, the machine didn't buzz.

I grabbed my jewelry and my suitcase, kissed Mom and Dad and Tim quickly, then dashed to the gate. Mr. List was waiting for me, and we hurried on board.

"I thought we were going to have to leave without you," Mr. List said.

"I know. Can you believe it, we left later than we'd planned and wound up being an hour late because of an accident."

I took a deep breath and handed my suitcase

to a flight attendant. *Well, anyway*, I thought, following Mr. List into the plane, *the rushing made saying goodbye easier*. I hadn't had time to get sad.

The plane was full. I scanned the crowd, searching for the familiar faces of my group. I heard some people speaking French, and I moved slowly down the aisle, looking for my seat, number 22A.

I found it and was startled to find that I'd be spending the next seven hours with none other than Henry Bouchet!

"You're sitting here?" I asked, trying to steady my voice.

"Yes," he replied blandly, his nose in a magazine. Then he looked up, and shock registered on his face as he realized who'd been speaking to him. "You're sitting next to me?"

"I thought I was going to be seated next to Tracy." I waved at her in the back of the plane.

"Are you sure you've got the right seat?" Henry took my boarding pass from me.

"What about you?" I demanded, annoyed that he would automatically assume I'd made the mistake.

After checking my pass, he looked at his own and then showed it to me. "Well, it looks like we're seatmates. Come on, hurry up. They generally like you seated for takeoff."

"Very funny." I plopped into my seat, exhausted already, and shoved my carry-on bag and purse under the seat in front of me. "I guess things got changed around."

Henry looked peeved, but I was sure he couldn't be half so peeved as I was. I buckled my safety belt, wishing I was with Tracy; I'd really been looking forward to gossiping with her.

Suddenly a flight attendant's voice came over the PA system, introducing the flight crew and giving the usual safety instructions. Pretty soon the plane taxied out to the runway, and in a matter of minutes, my stomach did a little flip-flop as we glided up into the air.

I looked out of the window, and while the ground dropped farther and farther away below us, I considered my predicament: I was going to be stuck sitting with Henry for about six hours, at least until we got to Zurich and changed planes for Bern. What do you say for six hours to a boy who constantly puts you down? "Have you ever been to Switzerland before?" I ventured.

"No, but I told you about my French relative in Switzerland, didn't I?"

I nodded.

"Well, he was my father's uncle, and he was part of the French resistance during World War Two and helped many people escape from France. Eventually he had to get out himself, and we believe he went to Switzerland, some-where around the Lake of Neuchâtel."

"Do you have any idea where?"

"No one knows. You see, lots of French people sneaked over the Alps into Switzerland at that time because it was a neutral country, but they still kept a low profile once they were there. They even lost contact with their families. Both my parents are dead, but I found out about my great-uncle from old letters and from my aunt."

"I'm sorry about your parents," I murmured hesitantly, feeling shocked by what I'd just learned. The funny, brave half-smile he gave made my heart go out to him. Suddenly I didn't think Henry had it as easy as I'd always imagined.

He shrugged. "Thanks. It happened a long time ago."

I wondered about him—was he trying to make up for something with his arrogance? That's the reason many people are boastful. But I didn't think Henry figured he had anything to make up for. Being orphaned so long ago probably didn't have anything to do with how he behaved now—although it did make me feel sad for him.

It wasn't easy to feel sympathy for Henry, though, because ever since we'd learned about the Switzerland trip, he'd begun teasing me more than usual. I always felt he was testing me somehow or trying to find out how bright I was, and that really made me nervous.

"How do you plan to find your uncle?" I asked, changing the subject.

"I'm hoping I'll be able to find something in the town records and libraries since he would have been a resident for many years now."

"Sounds exciting." We were quiet for a while, until I spoke again. "Who do you live with now?" I asked.

"My aunt and my younger brother."

"Did you learn French as a child?" I was really envious of Henry's pronunciation.

"No, I didn't know it as a child. I've taken just as many years as you have, but I guess I'm good at picking things up."

"You're good at being fatheaded, too."

He laughed. "I always had a special interest in French because my parents were French. They spoke it, and since they died when I was four, I look at learning it as unfinished business."

We pulled down the trays in front of us so the flight attendant could serve us dinner. I reflected on what Henry had told me about his family and tried to imagine what it must have been like for a four-year-old boy to lose his parents.

After dinner Henry brought out his French book and handed me a handwritten list from it. "These are some new words I thought I'd study during the flight. Want to quiz each other on them?"

I scanned the side of the page that had the words printed in English on it. *Analysis, valiant, idealistic, interwoven . . .*

"What will we use these words for, Henry? This isn't exactly your everyday vocabulary list, you know."

"I know. But it's always good to know extra words."

"Well, I don't know when we'll ever use them," I said huffily. "You probably dragged them out just to act smart. I know I'm not planning to get into an analytical discussion about idealistic values."

"Oh, cut it out." He laughed lightly. "So what if we don't use them? Our French will be better."

"Are you sure you don't mean cluttered?"

"You know most of the words necessary for simple conversation, but when you have to express your feelings, you're going to run into trouble."

"I can't wait to hear you use these words in a conversation," I said and giggled, imagining Henry getting all tangled up in his impressive vocabulary.

"If you're planning on a career with the UN, you'll need a bigger vocabulary," Henry said, folding his list and shoving it into his book.

"How'd you know that?" Henry was full of surprises, some of them unsettling, I realized.

He looked mysterious. "I have my ways of finding out. But when you do become a translator, you'll definitely be using words like these," he said with confidence.

I blushed. "Yes, but that will be years from now."

"And it will take years to get your French into the best shape. Foreign diplomats are not going to be impressed by your high-school French vocabulary."

"OK, OK. Hand me that list." I sighed loudly.

"Besides, Europeans are used to learning languages, whereas Americans don't generally go to the trouble. That means you'll have lots of competition out there."

"I know. I should've started learning when I was two."

"When you become a language star, you'll thank me." He handed me the list. "I can see the headline now: 'Robin Mackin Owes Success to Henry Bouchet for Broadening Her French Vocabulary During High School.' "

"You're impossible!"

"Really?" He leaned his head back against the seat.

My eye traced the line of his profile, the narrow nose, firm mouth, straight eyebrows frowning over dark green eyes. Maybe he sensed me staring because he turned to face me.

His steady gaze held mine. I was suddenly troubled by a fluttery sensation at the center of my chest, so I rooted around for something to say. "Speaking of ambitions, what are yours?" I asked. "I mean besides tormenting fellow French students."

"I'm not sure yet. I'd like to live in Europe, if I decide I like it. I know I want to do something that includes travel." He looked at me closely. "What nationality are you?" he asked.

The question came out of the blue and confused me. "American, of course," I responded automatically.

"No, no, I mean originally. You know, your grandparents or great-grandparents." He laughed, amused at my mistake.

"Oh." I blushed stupidly. "I'm a mixture of French, Danish, and Irish."

"You don't look too badly put together for someone with all of those foreign parts," he said, surveying me and grinning.

"I do all right," I said, ignoring his jab. "Basically, I'm hamburgers and french fries—American—like I said before."

"Well, let me show you some one-hundred-percent Swiss-blooded people. Here's the picture my host family sent me." Henry pulled out an envelope and took out a photograph. I leaned over and studied it. The Sardeaus had certain family similarities. Marie, the mother, was tall and dark-haired, as was her daughter, Elise. Her husband, Georges, was dark, heavyset, with a doughy face.

I pulled out the picture of my own host family, the Aubers, who had two children. The boy, Jerome, was away at college. Dominique was my age. She was petite and had chestnut-colored hair. Henry and I compared the photographs and talked about what we thought we'd feel about our respective families until the lights in the plane went off and the flight attendant announced that the movie was about to come on. It turned out to be a mystery, which took place in London and Paris. Henry and I sat quietly for a while, our eyes glued to the screen. Watching the winding cobbled streets shrouded in mist helped get me in the mood for Europe—not that I needed much help. But I imagined, as the hero sneaked past Notre Dame, the most important cathedral in Paris, that I was strolling hand in hand along one of those streets with someone special. Under an arched street light, we touched lips briefly, sending shivers down my spine.

"Are you cold?" Henry whispered, looking at me.

Boy, was I embarrassed. I'd forgotten about him, and he'd actually caught me daydreaming. "Oh, I guess I am," I mumbled.

"Let me get you something to cover yourself with." Henry got up and reached for the blanket in the storage compartment above our heads. I watched his muscles, taut beneath the long-sleeved shirt he wore.

"*Merci*," I said to him as he handed me the blue blanket and a pillow.

"You're welcome. We'll have to share it. There aren't enough to go around."

I had to admit there was something awfully cozy about sharing a blanket in the dark airplane, even with Henry. We drifted off to sleep, and I remember his arm next to mine on the armrest. I think I dreamed that someone was lazily stroking my hand. . . .

Chapter Five

I woke up just as the sun was rising, turning the clouds a gorgeous pink. Shortly after that we landed in Zurich to change planes for Bern. Mr. List looked tired as he herded us through customs like baby ducks. I guess it was really a big responsibility looking after six high-school kids in a foreign country. Since Zurich is in the German-speaking part of Switzerland, anyone in our group who had gotten lost would've been in real trouble. As I looked around, I realized how foreign everything was. I could imagine how E.T. felt when he was left on earth so far from home.

Melissa fell in beside me as we lined up at a newsstand to buy magazines and candy bars. "How're things going with Henry?"

"So far, so good," I said, shrugging. "I'm on guard." We peered out the big picture windows at the distant spires of Zurich. It was frustrating being so close to something new but unable to explore it. I turned around and saw Henry at a newsstand right behind us. He was buying a bag of peanuts and some French magazines.

"Hey, look, Robin. Henry's buying the *Paris Match* and some other magazines," Melissa noted. "I can't get over how good that guy's French is—he even *reads* in French for *fun*," she added.

I made a face.

"He's not an ogre, Robin. The way you act—I'm sure he thinks you don't like him."

"Well, he's got that right," I said, fuming. "Of all people to be seated next to on a transatlantic flight!" I would've continued complaining to Melissa about Henry and the flight, but at that moment Mr. List gathered us together and led us to a smaller plane, which would take us to Bern.

As we walked into the plane, Henry tapped my shoulder from behind. "Here's a magazine to keep you quiet," he said, handing me an issue of the French *Vogue*. "If you can't read it, you can at least look at the pictures."

"Did you get the magazine just to insult me, Henry?" I questioned.

"Hey, don't look a gift horse in the mouth, Robin." Henry scowled at me. "It might bite."

"Sorry. Thanks," I muttered grudgingly. Everything he said was a put-down.

Mr. List had given us our boarding passes in the Zurich terminal, and it turned out that once again I was to sit with Henry. I sat down next to him and opened the magazine. "I love fashion," I said. "It speaks its own language." I thought that sounded very profound, and I was just daring Henry to make some smart remark about it.

Henry smiled. "True." He glanced at the magazine, pointing out an outfit. "You should wear something like that." The model he was indicating was wearing a black jumpsuit and short black boots with the cuffs rolled down. Very chic. I wondered why Henry said that—was he trying to be facetious, or did he really mean that an outfit like that would look good on me?

I glanced at him, puzzled by his comment. Well, *was* it meant as a compliment? I hardly thought so. Henry didn't give out compliments often. He was too busy complimenting himself.

His presence completely unsettled me. One minute he was nice, and the next, he was beastly. I was expecting one of his biting comments every moment. Honestly, I hoped we wouldn't see much of each other on this trip. I decided to get a head start on ignoring him, so I turned away from him and looked out of the window.

The plane banked over the Alps, and we got a clear view of Bern ahead. It was an absolutely breathtaking sight.

And then, finally, we were there. After all the preparations, our trip was really beginning. We filed silently off the plane, all tired and, to be honest, a little frightened. I, for one, was wondering how I'd manage the language, the money, all the scary stuff I hadn't thought about much till then. Mr. List had assured us we could handle it. Other students had survived. But I was afraid, even though we'd gone through all the role-playing practices, that faced with any problem, I'd freeze up. I thought of Henry giving me a bad time about all this, and that made me even more nervous. What if I got all tongue-tied and couldn't say a single word to the Aubers. By looking at the long faces surrounding me, I could tell the others were having similar thoughts.

But once we were all packed together in the limousine to the hotel, we relaxed a bit. We peered out the windows for a look at our first Swiss city. Now I remembered some pertinent facts from our exchange-student meetings. Bern, the capital of Switzerland, is predominantly German speaking, though French, Italian, and Romansh are also understood there. As we drove through the beautiful Old City section, I recognized the Aare River, which I'd heard about, and marveled at the high-level bridges leading to the newer part of the city. There were lots of trams, motorbikes, bicycles, and cars crowding the streets.

"Now on the Junkerngasse," explained Mr. List as we drove into a street lined with older, arcaded homes. "These houses were once owned by the families of Bern." I remembered reading about this part of the city, but seeing it was another experience.

"There's the Bärengraben!" Melissa yelled.

"I'd like to see the bears," Tracey said excitedly. The Bärengraben, or Bear Pit, was an old moat in which bears have been kept since the fifteenth century. It's a very popular attraction.

"The Rose Gardens!" I said, pointing to Bern's rose gardens.

"I'm overwhelmed," Henry said simply.

At last we stopped in front of our hotel, a gray stone structure with ivy-colored sides. Everyone noisily piled out of the limousine. From the stares we got as we entered the lobby, we might as well have had the word *American* emblazoned across our chests. Mr. List spoke to the desk clerk in rapid French. Melissa whispered to John, asking him what was being said.

John shook his head, looking confused. Just to show off, Henry went up to the desk and asked about dinner. The desk clerk promptly presented Henry with a copy of the menu.

"Too bad we're not all whiz kids like you, Henry," I quipped. "Maybe we all ought to follow you around, then we won't have any language problems."

"That wouldn't be a bad idea," he returned, looking smug.

"OK, everybody," Mr. List said loudly, calling us to attention, "let's rest for a little while and freshen up. Then we'll have something to eat, and afterward we'll go to the bank to change our traveler's checks into Swiss francs."

Melissa, Tracy, and I went up to our room and began to unpack. Of course, we were all too excited to rest. We took quick baths in a funny, large bathtub, which had a hand-held spray nozzle instead of a shower head. We changed into fresh clothes, and within half an hour everyone was downstairs and ready for our first walk in Switzerland.

First we went to the subway station, and each of us was given a map of the subway system and shown how to use it. We took a ride to a different section of Bern, and after we'd walked around for a while, we realized how hungry we all were.

Mr. List led us to a tiny, picturesque café

where he made us order our own food in French. Melissa, who was really shy, got a little tongue-tied but managed to order bread and pâté.

Tracey couldn't stop giggling, and Dennis turned red, mumbling when it was his turn. John and I did pretty well. Actually, we all had more trouble understanding than we did speaking. Although we'd spent many hours listening to French tapes at school, we still weren't used to the Swiss dialect. Henry, of course, ordered his meal in perfect French with no problem whatsoever.

After lunch we all went window shopping. Under vaulted arcades, shops displayed wines, antiques, clothing, books, and sweets. After all our training with Swiss francs, Tracy still needed help counting out her money when she wanted to buy something.

"Tomorrow we'll see some monuments," Mr. List informed us excitedly. Monuments were his big interest.

"Isn't anybody tired yet?" Melissa complained, plopping herself onto a stone bench beside a sixteenth-century fountain we'd stopped to admire.

"No way, not yet," I said, still feeling exhilarated with the newness of everything.

"Hey," Tracy called, waving to a group of teenage boys across the street. We'd attracted their attention because we were obviously foreigners, and they were shouting "How's it going?" in French and grinning playfully at us.

"You're getting lots of attention," Henry remarked to me.

"All the Swiss look at Americans, don't they?"

"Especially American girls," he said. "You really stand out in your Levis and running shoes."

He was right. The clothes on the kids here were much different. Maybe it was just that they were city kids and we were from a smaller community. The girls wore skintight jeans with socks and pumps and baggy shirts or sweaters. The boys were, on the whole, more stylish than their American counterparts.

Eventually the Swiss boys wandered off, and Mr. List showed us a few more interesting buildings. By then we were finally feeling the effects of the long plane journey and our exciting, busy day. We were exhausted and more than happy to spend a few hours resting at the hotel.

As is customary in Europe, we had a late dinner at around eight o'clock in the plush hotel dining room. For an appetizer we were served liver pâté in a crock with a loaf of French bread and pickles. It was delicious, and I ate so much, I almost didn't have room for the main course: Wiener schnitzel, sliced carrots, and potatoes.

Salad came after that and then pastry and coffee.

"If we eat like this for three weeks, you'll have to roll us back on to the plane, Mr. List," Tracy said, and we all laughed.

"I think I'm in love with Swiss food," I said, leaning back in my chair.

"Your first romance, huh?" Henry ribbed me.

"It's probably a first for you, too, Henry," I shot back. I knew that the only way to deal with Henry was to give him a hefty dose of teasing back.

After dinner we all decided on a stroll beneath the Gothic spires of the Münster church, which was decorated with small lights at night. I don't know quite how we ended up that way, but Henry and I were walking ahead of the others up a small hill. From there we could see the Aare River curving like liquid gold around the old part of the city. Beyond, the outlines of modern buildings merged with the horizon, pinpoints of light glinting from their windows.

"This side of the river seems almost medieval," Henry commented, "while the other side has been hit by a giant dose of progress."

"The bridges look like diamond necklaces holding the two sections of the city together," I said.

"They do," Henry remarked, smiling at me, the darkness showing only a slice of his face. A

45

slight breeze ruffled his hair. Without facing me, he asked, "So how was your first day in Switzerland, Robin?"

"Wonderful!" I exclaimed, breathing in the strange, foreign-scented air. I couldn't describe exactly what it smelled like, but it was different and exciting.

"Do you think you'll come back?" Henryu asked softly.

"Why are you asking me that after one day here?"

"Maybe because I knew the minute we stepped off the plane that I wanted to come back." His eyes sparkled in the darkness.

I thought of what he'd told me on the plane about his family, and I realized Henry had a history here that I lacked. Naturally I was excited, but I wasn't searching for roots the way he was. Maybe that partly explained why he was so proud and cocky. French meant something special to him. It wasn't just a language, it was an understanding of the past for him.

As he gazed at me, I felt as though I had two sets of feelings about Henry. There were times, such as then, when I felt very warm toward him, then he blotted it out with his obnoxiousness, and I felt hostile toward him. It was confusing. I wasn't comfortable, really, with either feeling.

I was thinking of this when Henry touched my

elbow and said, "It's getting cold out here. We should go back."

His touch lit a spark in me, which was exciting and frightening at the same time. I flinched.

He shot me a look of confusion and quickly shoved his hands in his pockets. "Well, freeze then if you want," he muttered, his face growing dark before he turned on his heel and headed quickly for the hotel.

Had I hurt his feelings? I wondered, shivering suddenly. It was hard to believe Henry had feelings, but maybe I just preferred to think he hadn't.

Chapter Six

"Robin! Wake up!"

Melissa bent over me, her blond hair tickling my face. I blinked. This was Switzerland—and I was sleeping! I jumped up quickly. I didn't want to waste a minute. "What time is it? Have I missed anything?"

"Not yet, but you'd better get down for breakfast in two minutes. You know how eager Mr. List is to get to the monuments."

"Right." I could just imagine Mr. List's impatience if I held up the expedition.

"You're the last one up. Now hustle." Melissa started tossing my clothes at me.

I got dressed quickly, had breakfast with everybody, and started out, along with the rest of the group, for our second day in Switzerland.

That morning we saw more beautiful buildings and sculptures than I even knew existed. Melissa, Tracy, and I walked close behind Mr. List, so we could all hear everything he had to say about this beautiful city. Across the river, the glass-and-concrete facades of offices and apartments sharply contrasted with the quaint architecture of the Old City, where thick-walled stone houses boasted bright clusters of geraniums. Regional flags hung above shops, and many stores had two or three levels underground. Mr. List explained that strict laws limited buildings to four stories, so cellars had to be utilized.

A group of teenagers outside a cellar music store told us about a musical comedy they were going to see that night. They said it was something we shouldn't miss and that we could buy tickets inside the shop. We were all excited and hurried into the shop.

Later on we visited the Münster and rested a moment on its tree-lined terrace. Then we scaled the 254 steps to the tower, from which we could see across the entire city. The Clock Tower, once Bern's west gate, was our next stop. The east side of the tower had an incredible clock with mechanical figures that performed four minutes before every hour. Father Time with his hourglass, a jaunty merry-go-round of bears, a knight in armor, and a jester all danced merrily in the sunshine as they struck the hour.

A teenage couple stood looking at the clock and hugging. Watching them made my heart flutter.

After lunch our group split in two. Dennis, Henry, Mr. List, and John went to an art museum, while Melissa, Tracy, and I went to some shops to look at clothes. It was a great opportunity for us to use our French without Mr. List's help—or Henry's. But the most we could do on our own was ask simple questions of salespeople, and I had the frustrating feeling that I was being left behind by the fast chatter of French around me.

"*Combien est-ce?*" I asked the price of a pair of socks in a small men's clothing shop. I was trying to find a souvenir for my brother. It was hard because he isn't interested in anything but books.

"*Quatre francs,*" the little man replied. He held up three other pairs of socks to show me.

Four francs was too much for a pair of socks, and I looked to Tracy and Melissa for help, but they just laughed.

"You can handle this one on your own," Tracy said, giggling. "Mel and I are going out to get some *glace*. I'm starved!"

"Thanks a lot," I said. We wound up leaving the store together, but while Tracy and Melissa went in search of ice cream, I turned into the store next door. "I'll meet you two down the street in five minutes," I told them.

The shopkeeper I encountered in this store took pleasure in answering in English after I struggled to ask what other colors a particular blouse came in.

"So you can't pass for a native yet, Robin?" A voice behind me made me whirl around. Henry stood grinning at me with amusement. He'd caught me feeling very embarrassed, not knowing whether to go on with the conversation in French or in English.

"Why aren't you at the museum?" I asked pointedly.

He shrugged. "I got bored and thought I'd come out and deal with people instead of paintings."

"Now what color did you want? The gold looks nice." He held the blouse in front of me.

"Blue."

"Do you have this blouse in blue, madam?" Henry inquired in flowing French.

"Henry, you don't have to ask for me!" I hissed when the shopkeeper went to check her stock. "I can handle this."

51

"I'm just helping you out," he explained, but his interference made me burn.

I held in my anger while the shopkeeper showed me the blouse in the exact shade I'd wanted, but I just couldn't buy it under those circumstances. If only Henry hadn't helped me out—as though I couldn't do my own talking.

"It isn't quite the color I want, thank you," I told the shopkeeper in French—not as expertly as Henry would have, but it was good enough. She understood, nodded, and returned the garment to a nearby rack.

After we were out of the shop, I turned to Henry. "Why do you always have to act so smart? I get the feeling you're trying to upstage me."

"But, Robin, that would've looked great on you! Why didn't you take it?" he demanded.

"You heard me, Henry! It wasn't the right color." My throat felt tight, and I held back tears as I walked briskly ahead of him.

I strode quickly down the street to where Tracy and Melissa stood eating their ice creams. I was furious. It was difficult enough to speak French and figure out currency without being made to feel like an idiot about it. I put on a smile as I approached Tracy and Mel, but I could hear Henry's footsteps behind me.

"You really can't take any help, can you,

Robin?" Henry said as he got closer, his mouth set in a firm line.

"Not help laced with sarcasm," I hurled back.

Henry scowled and turned and walked away. I could tell by the stiffness of his shoulders that he was upset with me. But why? He was the one who was picking on me, making me look like a fool. I was simply the one reacting. Didn't he realize that when you hassle a girl she generally has something to say back? Or maybe he'd never read any of those books on how to win friends and influence people, I thought wryly.

That evening we all got dressed up. I wore a black-and-white-checked minidress with a gold belt. Melissa had on some satiny beige pants, and Tracy looked great in a new red jumpsuit. A day of checking out well-dressed shoppers had inspired all of us.

Henry was dressed in a brown sports jacket and slacks, and I had to admit that he really looked good, even though he glared at me when I entered the room. Dennis wore a rust sweater and cords, and John, whom we all worried about when it came to clothes, wore a sports jacket, too.

"Looks like they're trying to outdo us, doesn't it?" Henry addressed the boys while he surveyed us.

"That's easy enough to do," I said, but seeing his eyes darken, I wished I hadn't said anything.

"I'm proud to be seen with you," Mr. List exclaimed as he led the way to the theater.

The play turned out to be a fun, really great musical comedy about young love. I made sure I didn't sit near Henry, and I could sense him avoiding me, too. Yet my eyes strayed over his way once or twice. Looking at him troubled me, made me angry, and made me feel something else I couldn't define. Seeing his unhappy profile made me wonder if maybe Henry was right, maybe I really couldn't take any help. Maybe he'd been sincere in the afternoon, but I was so used to expecting sarcasm from him, that that's how I read it.

Once our eyes met briefly in the darkened theater, but I averted my gaze, suddenly feeling guilty, and didn't look his way again all evening.

The next morning we were up early and on the train for Neuchâtel. The ride was beautiful. Hedgerows and trees divided lush green fields. Farmhouses and small villages nestled snugly in the folds of the hills. As we drew near the Lake of Neuchâtel, the Jura Mountains rose sharply from the shore, majestic and overpowering.

"I'm looking at a living postcard!" I exclaimed. Henry sat in front of me. "Isn't this exciting?" He hadn't said anything offensive that day, so I thought I'd be nice to him. I noticed how his hair corkscrewed out from under the green beret he'd bought in Bern.

Whenever the train stopped, I occupied myself taking pictures. I felt as if I wanted to swallow the country whole in case I never got back again.

"Quick, take a picture, Robin," Henry said as the train wound around the lake and stopped at the little stone station in Neuchâtel. "Those people are probably our host families."

I snapped a picture while everybody else was disembarking, so I was the last one off the train. The families introduced themselves to us: the Sardeaus, the La Follettes, the Rabouds, the Vollys, and the Marchants. But the Aubers were nowhere in sight.

"Where is my family?" I asked Mr. List. I trusted that I'd recognize them from poring over their photographs. Just then Dominique came forward to greet me. Forgetting French altogether, I babbled in English, "Where are your parents? Is everything OK?"

Dominique smiled and spoke in halting, British-sounding English. I remembered Mr. List explaining that most of the English teachers in European schools were from Britain.

"My mother fell and broke her arm this morning and won't be able to have you stay for a week," Dominique said. "But," she added encouragingly, "when you do come, it will be so wonderful. Oh—I cannot wait! Anyway, until then Maman is very sorry but has arranged for you stay with our friends, the Sardeaus."

Elise Sardeau greeted me then and introduced her parents. "It will be wonderful to have you stay with us, Robin. We hope you'll be comfortable. We are Henry's host family and now yours, too." She smiled.

I nodded mutely and managed to smile back. I felt very let down, though. I'd prepared myself for months to meet and live with the Aubers. Mr. List must have sensed my distress because he wrapped a comforting arm around my shoulders. "Don't worry, Robin. I know this is a surprise to you, but it's only for a few days. Even though you don't know the Sardeaus through letters, I'm sure you'll be friends right away. And you'll have Henry to keep you company as well. Besides, we'll meet each morning at school, and I can help you with any problems you might have."

"Oh, I'm not worried," I exclaimed extra brightly, but the knowledge that I would be under the same roof with Henry suddenly hit me.

"Is this the realization of your wildest dream, Robin?" Henry teased.

"No, Henry, it feels more like I've just stepped into 'The Twilight Zone.' "

He laughed. "Well, think of it this way: you get to experience two Swiss households instead of one. And you'll have me close by."

"What a blessing," I said sarcastically. I bid the others reluctant goodbyes, particularly Dominique. She promised to seek me out at the Lycée Viñol.

"I will be very nearby," she assured me. "And I can't wait to get together to discuss clothes and music."

I laughed. I was looking forward to becoming friends with her. Suddenly Switzerland didn't seem so foreign after all!

Monsieur Sardeau drove beside the lake, then onto a curving drive that curled up the mountainside past many houses. He stopped in front of a massive stone château whose castlelike spires grazed a cobalt sky.

"So you live here?" I asked in French.

Seeing my surprise, Elise laughed. "Yes," she responded in French. "Where did you think? In the stables?"

It took me a minute to figure out what she'd said. Henry leaned over and told me that *les écuries* meant stables. Elise pointed to a barn, which actually didn't look like a bad place to stay.

As we walked toward the château, we learned from Madame Sardeau that the family had been vintners for years. Much of her conversation went past me, and I was grateful, for once, to have Henry nearby. "She says the land and the château have stayed in the family for a long time," he translated. "It's old and difficult to maintain. They should sell it, but they love it."

"I wonder if it has ghosts," I whispered.

"I wouldn't be surprised," he answered, holding open the creaking front door while I ducked under his arm.

The hallway was sparsely decorated with an antique table and chairs on a slick hardwood floor. Elise led the way up a spiral staircase to our rooms.

Henry pointed to the winding banister. "Looks like fun to slide down," he said to me.

I wondered if he was speaking to me now just because we were guests of the Sardeaus and it would seem funny not to. Or, he might think it was more sensible to attempt to get along since we had to live under the same roof.

I decided I'd go along with his game and be nice. There was no point in having the Sardeaus think we were both obnoxious.

"We'll really be welcome if you start sliding down banisters, Henry," I told him.

Elise showed me to a darling little room with

white-painted wood furniture and blue-and-white curtains. I stepped over to the window, which had a view of the gardens at the side of the house. Flowers were planted neatly in rows according to color so that they formed a rainbow.

"Do you want to see where I'm staying, Robin?" Henry called from my doorway.

"Sure."

He led the way down the hall and pushed open his bedroom door gently. "Now, isn't that fit for a prince?" he asked.

The room was done in browns and beiges. There was a model of a clipper ship on the dresser, and a Degas print hung over the bed. It was a perfect room for him, just as mine was for me.

"Nothing like getting the royal treatment," I said.

"No more than I'm due." He grinned and showed me to the window.

"It's a good thing they found a room big enough to accommodate your head, that's all I can say."

He laughed and showed me the view. Henry's room looked out over another carefully tended garden. Beyond lay the mist-enshrouded Juras.

A funny, melty sensation overtook me as I

stood near Henry, his breath brushing my hair. I shivered at his closeness.

He cleared his throat. "It's only midday. Let's unpack and relax a little. Then maybe we can go for a walk in the garden before dinner," he said.

I met his deep green gaze, and my heart jumped. I felt strangely drawn to him, but I also wanted to get away from him fast. "Sure," I mumbled. "See you later."

I was sure now that Henry was just trying to get along with me as best he could for the sake of our living arrangements. What other reason would cause him to start speaking to me after his silence of the night before? I tried to decide whether I liked it more when Henry was talking to me or when he wasn't. It was too confusing to figure out, so I went back to my room. I slipped out of my traveling clothes, sank into a warm, luxurious bath, and did my best not to think about Henry and the strange feelings he produced in me.

Chapter Seven

When Henry knocked on my door, he startled me awake. I'd fallen asleep in the overstuffed chair next to the window.

"We were going for a walk, remember?" Leaning his arms casually against the doorjamb, Henry looked amused. "You were really conked out. I knocked about ten times."

"I guess all this activity finally caught up with me."

"What'll you have to report when you get back to the US? We'll have to apologize for you—oh, sorry, Robin slept through that—"

"You just don't know when to quit, Henry, do you?" Quickly I combed my hair, then followed him into the hallway.

The downstairs looked more immense to me

than when we'd first arrived. We wandered around, not sure how to get outside. Luckily, a thin, birdlike woman who introduced herself to us as Yvette showed us to the front door, first asking if we wanted to eat something.

"No, *merci*," Henry answered for both of us.

"You didn't bother to ask me," I grumbled, knotting a scarf around my head. It was slightly breezy outside, though the sky was clear.

Henry stopped in his tracks. "Sorry, Robin. Would you like something to eat?"

"No, thanks, but I like to be consulted."

"I'm sorry, Robin, really," he said sincerely. We walked silently for a moment. Then Henry suddenly whispered, "Look at those birds. What kind are they? I've never seen any like them."

We stood still, not wanting to disturb the two brown-and-white birds in the slender tree in front of us. "There are so many things to look at and discover here," I said. "It's like being on another planet."

Henry nodded and then began to walk slowly around the gardens, marveling at the varieties of flowers. We stopped next to a small pond where goldfish slipped in and out of the water weeds. Henry dug in his pocket for a coin and tossed it in. "I remember once my little brother got on his hands and knees and dug all the money out of a fountain," he told me.

"What happened?"

"My aunt made him throw the money back in."

"Did he make a wish?" I asked.

"Lots of them." Henry laughed. Then his gaze moved from the pond to me. His hand brushed mine lightly.

Nervously I made a joke about how the house looked like a castle and how I should have a long, blond wig that I could send cascading down the stone wall of the building like Rapunzel's hair.

Henry didn't say anything for a moment, but he continued to stare at me in that intent way of his. I wondered what he was thinking.

"Sometimes you're awfully hard to figure out, Robin," he said.

I frowned, feeling uncomfortable under his scrutiny. "Why do you want to, Henry? Just so you can pick on me better?"

"I thought I was doing pretty well already! Ha, maybe I'll have to step up the campaign."

Heat climbed into my cheeks. Why were we at such odds? I just couldn't figure Henry out—or myself, for that matter.

"Oh, Robin, I just love your dress!" Elise exclaimed. She was wearing purple jeans with pumps and a loose gray sweater. She looked just like a Swiss teenager.

"Thanks," I said, making a note to buy a loose

sweater like hers. "I just bought this, and I wasn't sure if the stripes would be too flashy."

"Oh, no," said Elise. "It looks just right with your sandals, *très chic*."

Taking a last look in the mirror, I decided I really did look pretty good. My hair framed my face in soft curls, and a new bronze color eye shadow emphasized my brown eyes. Then I went downstairs for dinner, first phoning Madame Auber to see how she was doing. I told her in awkward French that I looked forward to seeing her and hoped she'd feel better soon.

The dining room was cozy, fire-lit, with thick red draperies held back by gold tassels, and heavy, dark furnishings. Henry was already seated. I noted, uncomfortably, that he looked handsome in a green sweater that matched his eyes.

We had french bread and liver pâté, then fish and some incredibly good Swiss-style potatoes and salad. I noticed that my conversation was limited to simple, but boring, phrases, such as "Please pass the bread," while Henry was able to hold a real discussion. Elise did not speak as much during dinner as American teenagers would. Her parents did most of the talking, as I learned was customary.

Madame Sardeau told us the dessert, *bagnolet crème*, was a specialty of the Jura region. It was a delicious anise-seed biscuit, stuffed with raspberries and cream. Henry wrote down the name so we'd know what to ask for the next time we ate out.

As Henry and I climbed the stairs to our bedrooms, I admitted, "You know, I feel like a little kid using such basic speech."

"But you're communicating. Isn't that what's important?"

"Yes, I guess so."

"You communicate facts well. The hardest thing to communicate is feelings," he said, squeezing my hand. "*You* should know that."

"What's that supposed to mean?" I said, on the defensive once again. I withdrew my hand, which was tingling from his touch.

"You have enough trouble communicating your feelings in English, let alone translating them into French."

"You don't know what you're talking about, Henry!" I cried in a huff. "Anyway, I'm sure I can communicate my annoyance with you in an instant, in any language."

He laughed. "That's for sure."

I scowled at him. He upset me at every turn. He was so arrogant it was maddening. How dare he presume to know what I was feeling and thinking? He would certainly be the last person on earth I would confide in, anyway!

*　　*　　*

The Lycée Vinol, our Swiss school, was a real surprise. Surrounded by expensive lawns, it was a gray Gothic structure with huge, echoing rooms. A reception for the American visitors was held in a long hall. The headmistress, Madame Orteau, was a small, efficient woman with gray-streaked, dark hair and a rather plain face. Her welcoming speech, from which I got the phrases, "Very pleased to have you here" and "We will help you however we can," Henry helped to translate for us.

"What would we do without Henry?" Mr. List asked.

Jealousy stabbed me as I glanced over at Henry's gloating face. Quickly I looked away and started formulating my next question for one of the teachers. I didn't want to waste too much energy on Henry. That would have made me madder.

Our first class of the day was homeroom with Mr. List, where we could discuss any problems we might have.

Melissa was upset because she'd overpaid for a scarf and didn't know whether or not she'd received correct change from another transaction. Dennis felt restricted with his host family. He had much more freedom at home. They didn't allow him to stay out late. Tracy reported that she'd gone to an ice-skating rink and eaten crepes with chocolate inside them.

The classes were noisier than American ones, and the teachers and students didn't relate to one another in the same friendly way they often do at home. I felt a little lost in the unfamiliar environment until I was made the center of attention in an English literature class, when I was asked to read a passage from *Huckleberry Finn* aloud.

After school Elise and Dominique gave Melissa, Henry, and me a tour of Neuchâtel. Dominique turned out to be an excellent guide. We'd corresponded for a couple of months, and now it was wonderful to fill in the details of her personality. She had a bright, cheerful way of leading the group around the sights, and though her English was more limited than Elise's, her descriptions were colorful.

Henry lagged behind in the old Collegiate Church, contemplating the fifteen paintings of the counts of Neuchâtel. "This is one of the finest Gothic memorials in the whole of Switzerland," he told me.

"Really? What page did you find that on?" I teased, pointing to his brochure.

"I learned it before we came," he returned huffily.

"Are you and Henry getting on better today?" Dominique took me aside to ask.

I laughed. "How did you know about my problems with him?"

"Elise said you were barely speaking, so we thought he was your boyfriend and you had had an argument."

"He's not my boyfriend!" I returned hotly.

Dominique giggled, and we all followed her down a stepped lane to explore the Renaissance fruit and vegetable market. "In the summer," she explained to everybody, "we have music all along the shore of the lake. Orchestras visit, and various concerts are held here. Last year famous rock bands, including the Rolling Stones, came here. And out there is where dances are held, and many kids like to roller-skate on the paths around the lake."

"Wouldn't it be great to be here in the summer?" Henry speculated. We looked out on the Lake of Neuchâtel, which shimmered in the afternoon sun. A few paddleboats and rowboats passed leisurely by, and we waved.

"I want to come back here someday," I told him.

He smiled down at me, his face made more radiant by the sun behind it. My heart pounded, and I shivered involuntarily. Oh, what was going on?

"Cold?" Henry inquired casually.

"A little," I replied. He didn't need to know that my shivers had nothing to do with the breeze blowing in from the lake.

"You can use my jacket if you want."

"You're being nice to me?"

"Yes, for two seconds, exactly. If you don't decide in half a second, the offer will self-destruct." He stared at his watch.

"I've never met anyone like you, Henry." His manner actually made me giggle. Boy, I never knew how I'd react to him from one moment to the next.

"And you never will. I'm one of a kind."

"That's a big plus for world peace, I think."

"I haven't yet told you exactly what I think of you, Robin Mackin." He said this in a surprisingly soft voice that caused something to stir inside me.

"Spare me," I bit back suddenly. "I think I can figure it out for myself."

Chapter Eight

No one was around when I returned to the Sardeaus' late the next afternoon, so I wandered into the study. The walls were lined with ceiling-high bookcases, filled with various volumes in English, German, Italian, and French. How wonderful it would be to speak all those languages! At sixteen, a Swiss student already knows one foreign language well and is beginning another. Of course, being multilingual is far more of a necessity in Europe than in the US. After all, countries are much closer together, and travel between them is as frequent as our travel between small New England states. Besides, in Switzerland alone, four languages are spoken.

There was a stack of books in the center of the

desk, and a few of them lay open. I started browsing through the open ones. They were about the French migration into Switzerland during World War II and about how the French Maquis helped people to escape from German-occupied France. Eventually, I read, these resistance fighters joined forces with the Fighting French to liberate France.

I read on, picking out a cardboard-bound manuscript, a college thesis entitled *Displaced French Families of WW II*. I leafed through the pages until the name Bouchet caught my eye. *Could this be Henry's family?* I thought excitedly, reading farther. "In 1940 many families fled their homes in Tour, France, to escape German occupation. Among them were the Brasiles, Bouchards, and Bouchets, who were members of the Maquis, or underground resistance. Later, they settled in the Jura region of Switzerland."

"There you are."

I whirled around, feeling a little like a child with her hand caught in the cookie jar. "Uh, hi, Henry. I was just looking at your books. Did you see this?"

He came over, read the page I had found, and gasped. "Wow, no. You just discovered this?"

"Yes. Where did you get these books?"

"I spent the afternoon in the library." Henry

flipped through the pages excitedly. "This might be a clue!"

"But does it tell you anything you don't already know?"

"I'm not sure." He put a finger to his lips, thinking hard. "In one of the other books, I read that there's a cave around here where French refugees stayed. I'd like to see it sometime."

"Sounds interesting."

"Maybe we could take pictures of it with your camera. And Monsieur Sardeau says there's a National Archives in Bern, but it might not be helpful since my family isn't originally Swiss. There's a great library in Geneva, too."

Was he asking me to go with him? I wondered. "Have you thought of writing to the town your great-uncle was born in for information?" I asked aloud.

"Those records were all destroyed during the war. They wouldn't do me much good, anyway, because they would be only birth records."

"What did your great-uncle do for a living?"

"He was a language professor."

"No wonder," I said aloud. His fingers accidentally brushed mine on top of the manuscript. I glanced down at the open text, our fingers spread on the sheet as if reaching across the pages. My skin tingled and felt hot before I yanked my hand away and tried to shove it in my pocket.

"You don't have pockets in those pants," Henry noted with amusement.

"You're right. I hardly ever wear these." I let my hands fall to my sides, feeling dumb.

"You know, I'm glad you're interested in these old books, Robin. A little education never hurt anyone."

I decided to ignore his comment. "My job at the library has me addicted to learning," I said, wishing my face wasn't turning bright red. "And besides, I might make somebody a really good research assistant."

I think I said that just to get back at him for making me feel like a dummy. A telephone call from Madame Auber saved me from getting into it any deeper with Henry. She said she planned to have me come to their home by the end of the week and was looking forward to having me. I hung up; the knowledge that I soon would be leaving the Sardeaus made a muddle of my emotions. Of course, I wanted to spend more time with Dominique, but I was feeling settled at the Sardeaus' home, and I sensed a softening, however slight, between Henry and me.

Maybe it was simply that I was aware of another side of him—nobody can be obnoxious all the way through, I decided. There's got to be something likable somewhere, though most of the time with Henry, it was hard to find.

Anyway, when he wasn't teasing me and making me feel like an idiot, we talked a lot about language and customs. French had become exciting to me in a new way, and I felt the need to talk about it to someone who was just as excited as I, and Henry was the only one. Could I be friends with Henry? Was that even possible? This was a question that confused me more than anything ever had in my life.

We were given a day off from school the next day, and Mr. List said we could use it by ourselves for "cultural enrichment."

Henry cornered me after breakfast. "Do you want to go to the library with me today, Robin?" he wanted to know.

"Which one?" I asked uncertainly.

"The one I told you about in Geneva. It'll be fun. Do you want to come?"

I wondered if it was a good idea. While Henry and I were around our group and the Sardeaus, he didn't give me such a bad time, but I was afraid that if we were alone he might subject me to his taunts. That would be a little hard to take, and I was tired enough already. I decided to make up an excuse.

"Well, I'm not really feeling too well. Maybe I'd better not go with you," I told him.

Henry's expression clouded over. "Sure, Robin," he said, as though he didn't believe me. "Well, if you have a sudden recovery, I'll be around for another hour." He whirled around and strode off.

I was confused—what did Henry expect of me? I was sure that the reason he wanted me to go was so that he could make me look small in some way. On the other hand, the trip sounded like fun. My first inclination had been just to go with him. After all, he *could* be nice at times. Well, it might be too late to change my mind anyhow; I suspected that he knew I'd made up an excuse.

I went outside to find Henry in the garden hitting croquet balls.

"When are you leaving?" I asked.

"Very soon. Why?" he responded coolly, not looking up from his mallet.

I took a deep breath. "Because I'm feeling better, and I'd like to go, if you still want me to." My words came out stiffly, and I felt embarrassed all of a sudden.

"OK. Let's get going." Henry smiled, and we went in the house to get ready to go.

We got to the station just as the train tore up to the platform, blowing my hair into a frenzy.

Henry and I found seats in a corner and settled down for the trip.

Terraced hillsides covered with vineyards rose sharply from the lakeside, blending with the Juras. Farther along the lake, little towns nestled on the shore. In the distance the Alps rose like icebergs above the rolling, green landscape, sending me digging in my tote bag for my camera.

Henry was very quiet and withdrawn during the trip, so I made a big thing out of taking pictures to try to get him to notice all the beauty passing by outside the window.

"Henry, look at that!" I cried. "Now isn't that just how you imagined Switzerland?"

"You sound like a tourist, Robin," Henry said, shaking his head. "Do you always take ten pictures of the same scene?"

"Oh, stop it! I want to make sure I get a perfect one."

"You must not have much confidence in your photographic abilities." He went back to reading his guidebook. He might be fascinated by facts, but I was much more interested in just looking around me. I took more pictures. It was a photographer's paradise. Each little village was more beautiful than the last.

At Geneva Henry and I bounded out of the train. When we were clear of the crowds, he buried his nose in the guidebook once more. "Now if we take this bus up to here, then walk here . . ." His fingers directed the way across the miniature map.

We ducked into a sweet shop and came out with a bag of Swiss chocolates, which we devoured on the way to the library. Usually I'm really careful about sweets, but these were too delicious to resist. Once inside the library, Henry quickly located the books he was interested in and handed me a huge stack. "I do feel like a research assistant all of a sudden. How much do I get paid for this?" I quipped, sliding my load onto the table.

We spent an hour plodding through old books and records. Every once in a while I glanced over at Henry, noting his complete absorption. His intense expression was highlighted by the shadow of the small reading lamp. I smiled as I sat looking at him. Maybe I was getting used to him, or maybe all the sugar in those chocolates had done something funny to my brain, but I actually felt warm toward him. I had no chance to analyze my feelings, however, because Henry turned to me, using his finger to mark his place in a book.

"Robin, I've found something." His voice was hushed, as though he'd just discovered a secret treasure. That low voice made me tingle. "My great-uncle died in 1976. He was a member of the Maquis, and he helped to liberate Paris in 1944. The rest of the family escaped before that, and he caught up with them later."

"Do you think they stayed in Switzerland after the war—France was really a mess. I remember that everything had been bombed really badly, and the factories had been taken over by the Germans."

"How'd you know that?" He viewed me with interest.

"My brother's college term paper. I helped him."

"I thought your brother was a brain."

"He is, but he can't type." We both laughed.

"Even lots of the railways were destroyed after the war. If the family was already settled in Switzerland, they wouldn't want to go back to a war-torn country." Henry snapped the book shut and looked at me. "What do you want for lunch?"

"Would you hit me if I said pizza?"

We walked outside and found a cute café decorated with potted flowers and tiny wrought-iron tables. They were so small that our knees almost touched. I sensed that the excitement at the library had made us forget we were enemies. We were having a good time at last.

A teenage couple sat at the next table, talking

in low tones. The boy had a handsome, craggy face, sort of like Henry's, and the girl had short, cropped blond hair. Every so often they casually leaned across the small table to kiss. Seeing their lips brush caused my heart to flutter. I thought, *I'm either going crazy or this is an awfully romantic place.*

Suddenly I wanted to bolt out of the restaurant. Henry, the couple, the heady romantic atmosphere wove a web around me that was nearly suffocating. I was afraid—what were my feelings? When I looked at Henry, I felt drawn to him, and I looked away quickly, not wanting to encourage my emotion.

Henry watched me watching the couple. I turned and addressed him hastily. "What will you do now that you know your great-uncle is dead?"

"Find out where the rest of the family is. They must be around here somewhere. According to that book, my great-uncle lived in La Chaux-de-Fonds, north of Neuchâtel."

"Are you going to go there?"

"Yes. I've come all this way, and I'm determined to find whatever's left of the family. Besides my aunt and brother, the relatives here are all I've got, Robin. I suppose I'm more involved with this project than most people would be because I don't have parents. When you've always had a family, you probably don't think about it much."

"You're right," I admitted. "I take mine for granted most of the time, but they're all right as parents go. We're a pretty close family." I sensed Henry and me getting dangerously close to some real emotions.

"You're lucky." Henry covered my hand with his. "I'm glad you came today, Robin," he said softly.

"Me, too," I replied, trembling at his touch and feeling both shocked and excited at the same time.

We finished our meal and strolled along the streets under the stubby stone towers of Saint Peter's Cathedral. I noticed that Geneva was more modern than a typically Swiss city. Henry pointed out the Jet d'eau to me, a pump-powered fountain of water that rises high into the air from a jetty extending into the lake. We stood near Lake Geneva and caught a distant glimpse of the famous peak, Mont Blanc, in the Alps.

A little bit later Henry and I entered a small clothing shop. I picked out a lovely multicolored shawl for my mother and a shirt.

"*Ça fait combien?*" I asked how much my purchases cost.

"*Quinze francs, mademoiselle.*" I was

relieved to find the shopkeeper answered me in French, especially since I felt nervous having Henry with me. As I was paying, an Englishwoman entered the store, looking very worried.

"Excuse me, have you seen my wallet?" she addressed the shopkeeper in a brisk, British-accented English. "It's brown with scalloped edging."

The shopkeeper shook her head in confusion and shot me a pleading look. "*Je ne comprends pas*," she said, meaning "I don't understand."

"This woman has lost her wallet," I managed in French, and I described what it looked like.

"Ah, *merci*." The shopkeeper clasped my hands in relief. Then she hurried to take down the Englishwoman's name.

Henry stood next to a rack of men's ties, and he smiled at me. "You were great," he said.

"Thanks, but I could've used you," I told him, remembering my frantic formation of an understandable sentence.

He shrugged. "You didn't need me, though. For once, I thought I should stay out of your way."

I didn't know what to say. It seemed as though, for the first time, he understood me. The thought sent trickles of warmth through me. As we walked together, Henry's hand brushed against mine, and I wondered what it would be like to have his arms around me. *For crying out loud*, I told myself, squelching the thought, *you're not even supposed to like Henry.*

We went into a watchmaker's shop, which looked exactly as if it had been lifted out of the movie *Heidi*. When we came out, I said to Henry, "I expected to see the hermit grandfather trudging down the mountain any minute."

Henry laughed. "It does feel as if we've walked onto a Hollywood set."

It was growing dark, and we stood for a few minutes, watching the sun sinking behind a shadowy horizon of buildings and streaking red fingers across the sky. Henry nudged me gently. "Come on. We'd better get home. The last train leaves at seven-fifteen."

On our way to the bus stop, Henry posed for me against a rail in front of a statue of a cherub, and I took his picture. "I've got a good name for you," I told him, smiling. "Henry the Poser."

"Wasn't there someone by that name sometime in the sixteenth century?"

We burst into laughter and didn't care in the least when the passengers on the bus stared.

The train was already pulling into the station when we arrived. Henry grabbed my hand, and we ran through the maze of hallways, down the stairs, and onto the boarding platform. The doors closed behind us as we leaped into the car.

It took us a few minutes to catch our breath. In the darkened window of the train, I glimpsed our reflections, faces flushed, eyes shining, hands still entwined.

Henry turned to look at me, and as I met his gaze, I felt something electric pass between us. After that moment, though, I wasn't quite sure I'd really felt anything at all. His hand slid off mine, and he turned once again to his guide-book.

Chapter Nine

"You've been daydreaming all day, Robin," Elise noted over lunch as we sat in the cobble-stoned courtyard at school. "Did you and Henry have fun yesterday?"

"Yes. Henry found some information about his family." I kept remembering how Henry had looked, how he'd understood enough to stay out of the way when I helped the shopkeeper and the Englishwoman. And when he took my hand . . .

"I think you and Henry make a nice couple," Elise told me in her precise English.

I looked away, but my bright cheeks betrayed me. Had I just been thinking the same thing, but in a more roundabout way? How could I? Just the day before I had been making up excuses not to be with him, and now. . . . "Hmmm. He seems different since we got here," I admitted.

"You were not friends when you arrived?"

"We were in French class together, and he was always a real' nerd, always trying to outdo me. I sure wasn't happy to learn we'd be staying in the same home together."

"Nerd?" Elise looked questioningly at me.

"Not a nice person" was all I could think of as a translation. It was hard to remember not to use American slang, but the Swiss kids at our school seemed to enjoy learning it, nevertheless.

"Then Henry is not, as you say, a nerd," Elise said, "because he is a nice person. Handsome, too. I wish I had a boyfriend. Have you ever had one?"

"Not a real one. I've just dated a little, nothing serious."

"Do you want a romance?"

I thought about that for a moment. Romance had been on my mind lately, even though I didn't really know what to expect of it. I remembered Henry's and my reflections in the train window. Did I dare think that we might look good together? Or maybe it was just my crazy heart playing tricks on me, making me think of Henry in a different way now. Maybe Henry was just being nice to me because we were both living in the same home. Yet in Geneva, after we got over the initial awkwardness, he really was friendly, and everything had worked out wonderfully. Did he think so, too?

"Well, someday I would like a romance," I told Elise dreamily.

"Maybe Henry does, too." Elise suggested, biting into her sausage sandwich. "I liked a boy last year," she said. "But I liked him too much. Maman told me not to chase him, but I didn't listen to her. I thought I had to let him know how much I liked him. Yet, still he wasn't interested."

"How could he not like you? What's not to like?" I demanded.

She shrugged, tossing back a lock of thick, dark hair. "I don't know. Maman says I need to learn not to appear so anxious."

"Were you in love with him?"

"I think so."

We finished lunch, and Elise distributed part of a leftover sandwich to a flock of pigeons. She went back to school, and I joined Mr. List and the group for a tour of the church of Saint Pierre de Clages.

As I walked around the Romanesque church, my conversation with Elise nagged at me. How *did* I feel about Henry now? Now that I knew another, warmer side of him, and now that he had swept me up in his quest for his family. And in Geneva he hadn't made me feel like an idiot when I had spoken French. That was a major breakthrough, I thought.

That evening Dominique Auber took Henry and me to a rock concert held in the school gym. It was not so large as most American rock concerts, I told Dominique when she asked how the concert differed. I was also surprised to find programs given out at the door.

"We don't throw paper airplanes, either," Henry said, referring to the folded programs sailing past our ears every few seconds.

"We throw Frisbees, instead," I said.

Henry disappeared for about fifteen minutes after the concert, and Dominique told me about the last time the Rolling Stones had played in Switzerland and how big the crowd was. Then she looked thoughtful.

"You know, Robin, I think Henry likes you, but he thinks you don't like him."

"Are you kidding?" I asked in disbelief. "Why does he give me such a hard time then?"

"You make him behave that way. He feels he has to prove something, be better always, and especially he feels that you don't like him."

"Well, he could be right. He makes himself hard to like, with his attitude," I complained huffily.

Henry returned with two programs, one for me and one for Dominique.

"Here. They're autographed," he said, handing them to us. I opened mine. It read, "To Robin, best of everything, Jean-Pierre Balsac," in French.

"*Merci*, Henry," I told him, so overwhelmed I didn't know what else to say.

"You're welcome." He grinned.

Dominique winked at me. I blushed. Maybe she was right after all.

When we got home, there was a letter for me from Lacey on the hall table. It said:

Dear Robin,

We miss you, but things are going pretty OK here. Michael and I broke up. He wants to date other people. Does the course of love ever run smoothly? I'm all confused. Sure I can date other people, but I don't feel like it. I think I gave Michael my heart and won't ever get it back.

Well, anyway, enough of the depressing stuff. From your postcard it sounds like you're having a great time. I hope you're having fun with H.B. Being under the same roof with him must be crazy. Oh, well, maybe you'll find he's not so bad after all. Write soon.

Miss ya,
Lace.

My heart went out to her. I realized I had been doing a lot of stretching lately to accommodate all my many new feelings.

"Did you know that La Chaux-de-Fonds is the capital of the watchmaking industry?" Henry informed me at breakfast.

I broke my croissant into two pieces, watching the little flakes drop all over my napkin and plate. "Wow, that must be the most amazing thing I've ever heard," I said teasingly.

"It's important to know these things, Robin," he said, sounding like a teacher. "Hey, guess what? Mr. List said I could get some extra credit for my research on my relatives! He's been helping me a lot and been a real inspiration to me!"

"That isn't fair. The rest of us don't have special projects like you," I blurted out, unable to contain my jealousy.

"Gee, I'm sorry, but I really have been putting tons of work into it. Mr. List says I've learned a lot."

Great, I thought. *Mr. List is so interested in you he doesn't have time for the rest of us.* "You don't really need the attention, you're the best student in the class."

"I know," he said, sighing. "It's a trial carrying that distinction. But seriously, I'm going to the genealogical records center in La Chaux-de-

Fonds today as soon as we get out of school. Will you come with me?" Henry asked. "Maybe I can find out who my cousins are from the birth records."

I took a moment before answering. "Sounds interesting. Sure, I'll go."

Henry and I sat close together on the train. I'm not sure whether this was by choice or because we were sandwiched between a large woman with two toddlers on one side and a businessman smoking a cigar on the other. Anyway, I liked being close to Henry. In fact, I just plain liked being with him, I finally admitted to myself, even though he did still bug me a lot.

As planned, we went to the genealogical records center in La Chaux-de-Fonds, which is a town in a high valley of the Juras above Neuchâtel. It was here that Henry finally found what he wanted. "Paulette and Edouard Bouchet, born to Maurice and Paulette Bouchet, July 26, 1955," Henry read off the microfilm. "They moved to Lausanne in 1970. I wonder if they're still there."

"Let's look in the phone directory," I suggested.

"Hmmm." Henry didn't answer. He was glued to the screen like a kid watching a video game.

I went to the pay phone and dialed Lausanne

information, bravely quelling my fear about speaking French on the telephone. My nervousness was unfounded, anyway. The operator understood me perfectly and gave me the information I needed right away. It turned out that there was an Edouard Bouchet living in Lausanne. I wrote down the number and silently handed it to Henry.

"I'm phoning them," he announced impulsively. I watched the excitement mount on his handsome face as we crossed to the phone and then as he spoke in flowing French to his cousin. He turned to me, flushed, as he hung up. "We're invited over there tomorrow afternoon. Isn't that great? Aren't you excited?"

"Excited for you," I said, smiling. I was getting a real sense of history going through this with Henry.

"If you don't want to go, I'll ask Mr. List," he said hesitantly.

"No, I want to go!" I insisted.

Henry flapped his arms around like Big Bird. He was so happy he actually started to giggle. "C'mon. Let's go walking by the park."

We strolled by a huge, well-shaded park. Older people were playing cards and chess there, while some teenagers were kicking around a soccer ball. Henry and I joined them and came away winded, complaining about what experts they were.

Afterward we rewarded ourselves by sharing a sandwich at a sidewalk café. I couldn't believe how much fun I was having with Henry. A group of kids around our age sat down at the table next to us and pointed out the best things on the menu. They also mentioned a concert they thought we might like to go to in town.

"Talking Heads are playing here, can you believe it?" Henry laughed. I noticed how cute he was when he thought something was funny. "Everyone here is so excited about American music. Now why would they tell us to see an American group in Switzerland?"

"It's their attitude that everything American is better," I said. "Even if they don't understand the words to the songs, they're more excited by them just because they're American."

Henry watched me. Gently he wiped a tiny spot of mustard from my cheek. "Thanks," I said. "I really get into my food."

"So I noticed." He chuckled. "Guess we won't be needing a doggie bag." We laughed, argued over who was paying the bill, and ended up splitting it.

"You know, we don't have to rush back to Neuchâtel right away," Henry said, smiling at me. "We could spend the rest of the afternoon here and catch a train back in the evening."

"Great," I said, smiling back. "Let's stay awhile. What do you feel like doing?"

"Hmmm. Why don't we browse in some shops and then see a movie?"

I nodded happily, and we were off, searching excitedly for stores. Henry wound up liking the watchmakers best. I looked at clothes and souvenirs, trying to find things I might take home to my family. Then we went together into a shop that sold music boxes.

"Oh, look at that one!" I exclaimed, pointing to a heart-shaped box with a boy and girl hand in hand on top, gazing at each other.

Henry wound up the box. "That's a pretty tune, isn't it?"

"It's beautiful," I said, my voice catching in my throat as I watched the boy and girl twirling around.

"Why don't you get it?"

I shrugged. "I still need to get something for my father. I've got to watch my money," I announced practically.

"Come on," Henry said and patted my shoulder. "Let's see what's playing down the street."

We went to see an American movie, which we'd both seen before in the US, with French subtitles. The theater had reclining seats, and snacks were brought around to everybody. It was fun not having to get up at intermission to buy popcorn.

We rode the train back to Neuchâtel, each lost in private thought. At our stop Henry took my hand and held it as we strolled through the darkened streets to the Sardeaus'. Halfway up the drive, he turned to look at me. I was struck by how different he looked at that moment. The same face I had once thought so arrogant seemed attractive and familiar.

Henry's arms closed about my waist, and he pulled me toward him. As he kissed me, I melted like butter. I wanted the moment to last forever. I wanted to feel the warmth of his embrace always, his lips never leaving mine.

"I've waited for this moment for a long time," Henry whispered in my ear.

"Really?" I wondered if Henry had secretly cared about me all this time, during which, I now realized, I had cared about him. This was a dream, it just couldn't be.

"Yes. I can't believe that tomorrow I'll be seeing members of my own family."

My heart sank. I felt as if I'd been dropped from a three-story building. It wasn't me he cared for, he was just happy about finding his cousins. I was trying desperately to recover from both the

kiss and the fact that it obviously meant something very different to Henry than it did to me.

"Robin." He said my name so softly, so
urgently that my heart ached. "Do you understand how this feels to me?"

"I'm trying," I said, pulling away from him to
walk up the hill, my footsteps echoing loudly.
The darkness, which a moment ago had seemed
romantic, now felt very lonely.

Henry was running to catch up with me. He
took my elbow and gently spun me around. "Can
I kiss you again?" he asked.

"Did you ask the first time?"

"I can't remember."

He rubbed his nose against mine, kissed me
tentatively, then more passionately, making me
think that he might care for me after all. I
stroked the back of his neck softly. Suddenly I
remembered something Lacey had written in
her letter. "I hope you're having fun with H.B.
Being under the same roof with him must be
crazy. Oh, well, maybe you'll find out he's not so
bad after all."

Chapter Ten

I was surprised early the next morning before breakfast to get a telephone call. It was from Madame Auber.

"*Bonjour,*" I greeted her as I picked up the phone. I had called her several times while I was staying with the Sardeaus so that the Aubers and I would feel more comfortable with each other when I finally went to stay with them.

Madame Auber told me her arm was much better and that she was, at last, ready to have me stay with her family. She said that I should make plans to move to their house as soon as possible.

I slumped down on the curved loveseat next to the phone, my heart thudding in my ears. I had to leave the Sardeaus—which meant leaving

Henry. I knew we wouldn't see as much of each other if we weren't in the same household.

I wondered how he would behave toward me that day. *He must like me*, I thought, remembering our kiss. Unless maybe he'd just been swept away by the moment. Maybe he would kiss anyone under those circumstances, even a toad. I frowned.

Oh, what was really going on here? After all the bad feelings I'd had about him, it was hard to imagine Henry liking me. But now I had to consider all the time we'd spent together recently. I really had wanted to be close to him since we'd arrived in Switzerland. Did he want to be near me, too? And why? We picked at each other nonstop. But I knew a different Henry beneath the tough, prickly surface now. And, I admitted to myself, the real me was pretty different from the surface me I presented to the world, too.

When I looked deep inside myself, I saw a girl who was not always tough and brave, who wasn't as good a French student as Henry was, but tried to act like it anyway. But most clearly, I saw a girl who was awfully vulnerable and who thought about falling in love a lot. I wondered whether Henry knew that last bit about me. I hoped I wasn't that transparent.

But what about him? I thought about Henry's

parents dying when he was young and how that loss would have shaped him. Perhaps he was making up for that loss by trying to be the greatest. Maybe he needed to think he was superior just because if he didn't, nobody else would.

In some ways, I guessed, I was a little like Henry. I didn't want anyone to see where I was weak, so I covered it over with jokes and sarcasm.

I went downstairs, imagining what Henry would do when he saw me. Would he try to kiss me when no one was looking? Would he touch my hand, hug me, wink at me, give me any sign at all? Or would he act as if nothing had happened? My hand trembled as I reached for the double doors of the dining room. But when I entered, Henry wasn't there.

"Is Henry coming down to eat?" I asked Yvette nonchalantly in French as she placed scrambled eggs in front of me?

"No. He left early this morning with Monsieur List."

"But we were supposed to—" I broke off in the middle of the sentence. This was the big day when Henry would finally meet his relatives. We were going to go—together. Why hadn't he woken me?

"Weren't you meeting Henry today, Robin?" Elise asked as she entered the dining room.

"We were planning to go to Lausanne together, but he's already left. I thought we'd be leaving in the afternoon." I swallowed my disappointment and hoped it wasn't showing all over my face. "He went with Mr. List instead."

"That's too bad," Elise said gently. "Do you want to rent a rowboat and spend this lovely Saturday on the lake?" she asked sympathetically. "If we do go, we should get back early, though, because Mr. List is coming for dinner and Yvette has planned something special."

"Well, that sounds nice," I said, trying to be enthusiastic. I certainly wasn't going to sit around doing nothing all day. But why had Henry decided to go to Lausanne without me? I wondered, feeling hurt. He'd joked about taking Mr. List, but hadn't I made it clear that I wanted to go?

"When Henry gets back—" Elise began, but I interrupted her.

"We don't know when he plans to get back, and I'm not waiting for him, Elise. Let's go rowing." Elise didn't say anything and shrugged.

The lake was beautiful. We rowed out to the middle, then just drifted. "This is very peaceful," I said, lying on my back, my face toasting in the sun.

"I'm sure there's a good reason why Henry left without you, Robin," Elise said, trying to console me. I smiled weakly at her. "You know," she added impulsively, "I'm going to miss having you stay with us."

"Me, too. You're like a real sister to me."

"And you don't want to leave Henry," Elise said understandingly.

"I couldn't care less about Henry right now," I said harshly.

"You didn't feel that way yesterday," she reminded me.

"No, but today everything has changed."

"Everything can't change in one day, Robin. You were floating on a cloud yesterday. Now you're sinking in—how would you say it—quicksand? All because of Henry." We laughed and started rowing, the water making little slapping sounds against the hull of the boat.

The time passed peacefully for me in the boat with Elise, but I couldn't help wishing I were with Henry, even though I was furious with him. I tried to think of some logical reason why he'd stood me up, but I couldn't. I figured he'd decided he just didn't want me around. Our kiss had simply been a mistake. He hadn't meant what that kiss implied.

The day went quickly—probably because I was thinking so hard—and when the air began to get cool, Elise and I returned the boat and walked home.

When we got to the Sardeaus', Henry and Mr. List were in the drawing room. "*Bonjour*, Robin, Elise," they chorused.

"Hi," I replied airily. "How was your day?" I smiled at Mr. List but avoided Henry's eyes.

"*Très bien, merci*," Henry replied coolly. "Where were you today, Robin?"

"You weren't here when I got up, so I figured you'd gone to Lausanne without me." I tried to sound casual, but instead I sounded like a petulant baby.

"I went out to breakfast with Mr. List and a man who thought he knew my family in Lausanne, but it turned out to be a different Bouchet family who had also originally emigrated from France."

"Really?" So Mr. List was helping Henry, the ultimate pet student, after all. All Henry really wanted, more than anything else, was to locate his family. And Mr. List could help him do it. Nothing else mattered. He hadn't even bothered to tell me about his change of plans. Instead, he'd stood me up. My throat felt dry and scratchy, and I could barely get my words out. "I know how badly you want to find your family, Henry." He shot me a look of confusion at the strained tone of my voice. "Would you excuse me?" I requested coolly. "I have some things to do upstairs."

With that, I fled up the steps, and before I reached the second-floor landing, tears formed two thin rivers down my face.

I'd been an idiot for thinking Henry cared about me at all! Well, thank goodness, I was going to the Aubers' the next day. It would be easy to stay out of his way once I was there.

Angrily I shoved clothes into my suitcase every which way, sweeping the dresser clear of my belongings, except for the toothbrush and comb I'd need the following morning. I never wanted to lay eyes on Henry Bouchet again, that was for sure.

Elise came in and put a comforting arm around me, setting loose a new flow of tears. "Robin, do not be upset. Henry did not mean to hurt you."

"But he didn't apologize for this morning, or anything—" I choked on a sob, feeling horribly sorry for myself.

"Look, rest now. We have a special dinner tonight. You will feel differently later," she said, smoothing my hair.

But at dinner time I claimed I had a headache and spent the evening in my room. I heard Elise knock softly at my door, but I pretended to be asleep. It was much easier that way.

"Aren't you saying goodbye to Henry?" Madame Sardeau asked me in French. She scrutinized me carefully as I plunked my suitcase down in the foyer.

I avoided her gaze, concentrating on the flowered carpet. "I'll let Elise do that for me," I said stiffly. "I really must go. The Aubers are expecting me."

Elise and I climbed into the backseat of the car and exchanged knowing glances as we peered up at Henry's bedroom window. I wondered if he would be up yet and notice me leaving, and I wanted him to lean out of the window and shout, "Robin, please come back!" like in a movie, but naturally he didn't. Those things just don't happen in real life. Henry slept through my departure, not knowing a thing about it.

I hugged and kissed all the Sardeaus when we parted in the Aubers' front hall. "*Je reviendrai*," I told them, "I'll come back."

Madame Auber was in her midforties. She had chestnut hair streaked with gray; a handsome face, and cream-colored skin. "We'll take good care of Robin, don't worry," she smiled at the Sardeaus, patting my hand in a motherly fashion. Monsieur Auber, a tall, gray-haired man with sharply chiseled features, had an intriguing way of gliding when he walked. Of course, I already knew Dominique. She stood next to her father, smiling comfortably, her bright chestnut hair and lovely skin echoing her mother's.

They were very all kind to me and made me feel at home immediately. I felt bad about having to force my smiles. The mood I was in made my French come out atrociously.

Just after the Sardeaus left, the phone rang. It was for me.

"Why did you leave without saying goodbye?" Henry's demanding tone made me suddenly breathless.

"I didn't—"

He cut me off before I could explain. "Since I didn't get to meet my cousins yesterday, I thought I'd set up another time to meet them. I'd like you to come with me. That is, unless you're not interested. The way you're acting, I wonder if you are at all."

Now I was furious. He hadn't even apologized for standing me up the last time, and now he expected me to make another date with him! "You're right, Henry. I'm not the least bit inter-ested," I announced coldly and slammed down the receiver.

I wasn't going to give him any more chances to upset me. When I looked down, my hands were trembling. I stuck them in my sweater pockets to keep them still, but that didn't quiet the pounding of my heart.

Chapter Eleven

The Aubers' home was a modern, slope-sided chalet nestled in a hillside. A wood stove stood on one wall of the living room. Thick, hand-woven rugs were spread over the hardwood floors. Blankets were thrown over each piece of overstuffed furniture. It seemed like a cozy place to curl up on a chilly evening.

At school Dominique and I had gotten to know one another pretty well before I moved in. We had common interests in clothes and music.

"I just love American rock groups!" she exclaimed excitedly, showing me her room, which was decorated with posters. Then she brought out her French and British record albums for me to look at. I noticed that the artwork on the record jackets was really different from the artwork on American albums.

"When I come to America, can I see a concert?" Dominique asked eagerly.

I loved her enthusiasm about things. She really was adorable. "Oh, sure. I'd love to take you. We'll go see whoever's around."

"I am so excited about the visit. Maybe you will invite Henry to come with us, too."

"Henry? Ha! If we're speaking to each other then," I scoffed, fresh hurt filling my eyes.

"Oh, Robin. Henry likes you so much. He is, how do you say it? Very cute." She elongated the word "cute" in an attractive way.

"If he likes me, then why doesn't he show it?" I challenged.

"Henry is prideful. He is covering a soft spot. He may be afraid to admit he likes you," Dominique ventured.

"I thought so yesterday, but today, I think he's just a jerk," I said with conviction.

"Jerk? Is that American?"

Dominique seemed to enjoy Americanisms. "Yes." I giggled. "Henry is an American jerk, and he bugs me."

" 'Bugs you'? I love that—I never learned that expression."

"It means to annoy."

We went through my clothes as we hung them up and then examined Dominique's wardrobe.

"You need tighter, shorter jeans like these," she said, holding up a pair of her own. "You mustn't wear those loose ones. They are not chic."

"You'll help me shop for them?" I was excited at the prospect and pleased at Dominique's interest.

"Oh, I would love to." Dominique was enthusiastic. "And I want you to help me shop for makeup in America. Here it's not customary for girls to use makeup until they're much older, yet we all love it."

That night Dominique took me to a Swiss disco with a group of her friends from school. I was not surprised by the music—as I'd expected, it was predominantly American. I danced with a few boys, remembering what it was like to dance with Henry. How it felt to be in his arms, his hands on my back, pressing me closer, his warm breath against my ear.

I pulled away from my partner, a thin, shy boy who was a head shorter than I, and thanked him for the dance.

I thought that the lights and music at the disco would help me forget about Henry, but instead the atmosphere made me think of him more. Dominique danced for most of the evening with a boy named René, whom she recognized from school. When we went home, she was ecstatic and couldn't wait to see him again the next day at school.

But school was the place I least wanted to go to the following morning because that was where I'd see Henry, and I didn't know how I was going to deal with him.

I wound up avoiding Henry completely at school, and later during a group excursion to a *fromagerie*, where cheese is made, I made a point of not looking in his direction—though I did see enough of him out of the corner of my eye to note that he seemed to be avoiding me, too.

Anyway, the *fromagerie* was interesting. We watched cheesemakers cooking batches of fresh milk in giant vats and cutting the curds with wire paddles that looked like miniature harps on sticks. Later, they hoisted the curds out in huge cheesecloth nets and molded them, under pressure, into huge cakes. Our guide explained to us in French that after two weeks of daily washing with saltwater, the wheels of Gruyère cheese would travel to an underground warehouse in another town for six to ten months of aging. I was fascinated by the process and also very impressed with myself for understanding the explanation in French so well.

I left the *fromagerie* and headed back to my

new home quickly so I wouldn't have to talk to Henry. Then I went out for a walk on the slopes behind the Aubers' house. It was a good, quiet place to think.

I realized that my experience with Henry in French class back in the States should have been enough of a warning of what he was really like: arrogant, boastful, and argumentative. I should have trusted my first impressions. Instead, I'd allowed myself to be fooled into thinking he was different or that I simply hadn't known him before. Well, now he was showing his true colors once again. I puffed up the hill slowly, so engrossed in my thoughts that I barely noticed the beauty around me. How could I ever have thought Henry cared for me? Why was it, I asked silently, knowing how hypocritical I sounded to myself, that in spite of my efforts not to like Henry, I still kept thinking about him?

I rounded a bend in the path, and a breath-taking view of Neuchâtel greeted my eyes. The tall, pointed roofs of the storybook town were diminished to dollhouse proportions. I stood still, drinking in the scene. My heart ached, and I wished Henry were with me. But why? I was furious with him! Before we'd spent any time together, I was able to visualize myself with a boy, but he was a faceless person, a dream. But now, Henry's face filled in the blank. I had to admit that my feelings were real—whether I wanted them or not.

I'd allowed myself to think Henry was different, that there were real reasons for his pride and arrogance, and that I should be tolerant. Now I was stuck liking him. Dominique might think he liked me back, but I expected him to show it in a different way. Maybe he'd only wanted me to help him find his family, and now he didn't need me anymore. He really wasn't interested in me just for myself.

After a while I trudged back down to the house. Mr. List phoned, looking for Henry.

"I haven't spoken to him all day," I told Mr. List.

"Too bad," he said, sensing the tension in my voice. "You know, Robin, on Saturday I called for Henry to meet the man he told you about. He was going to wake you but decided not to since you two had been out late the evening before. But Henry went back to the house for you after breakfast, and you weren't there. He was very upset to find you gone."

"Came back? For me?" I questioned in disbelief. "Why didn't he say so? Why didn't he explain things? Didn't he know that I thought he'd stood me up?"

"I think he felt *you* stood *him* up, that you

didn't want to go to Lausanne with him," Mr. List explained noncommitally.

Henry really thought that? I wondered, letting the thought register. How could he? Didn't he know how interested I was in him? How much I liked him?

I said a hasty goodbye to Mr. List and hurried to check the Sardeaus' telephone number. I wanted to kick myself for not seeing this before. My anger was dissolving fast. I really had misjudged Henry.

"Such a rush?" Dominique questioned me when she saw me dialing the phone in a frenzy.

I nodded and smiled, not having time to think up a French response. All I wanted to do was talk to Henry.

Elise answered the phone. "I missed you at school today," she remarked somewhat wistfully. Unfortunately in order to avoid Henry, I'd had to avoid Elise that day.

"I'm sorry, too," I said. "Listen, Elise, I have to talk to Henry."

"You two are making up, I hope?" she asked.

"Oh, I hope so, too, Elise."

"But he is not here, Robin. He's gone to look at a cave where his great-uncle stayed during the war. Do you know it?"

I remembered Henry telling me about the cave. It was located above Neuchâtel between the

Sardeaus' and the Aubers'. "Sort of, but I'm not exactly certain where it is."

Elise gave me clear instructions. "When the road forks, take the lane to the right. You'll pass three farmhouses but keep going. It's in a cluster of trees. Walk toward them, and soon you'll see the mouth of the cave."

"Thanks."

Elise sounded thoughtful. "He should have been back a long while ago, Robin. I hope you find him."

It took me awhile to get to the mountainside, and when I did, the climb was steep. A narrow, rocky trail wound up past a few slope-roofed farmhouses. I was thinking that Henry probably wouldn't even want to speak to me after the way I'd acted. I had been so silly in so many ways—especially being envious of his relationship with Mr. List. After all, what teacher wouldn't be interested in Henry and his search for his family? And Mr. List had always been very encouraging to me, so I had no reason to feel jealous.

The darkness deepened around me. In the distant west, the sunset painted the sky in vibrant orange and pink splendor. Mist clung to the ground, gradually thickening into fog. I spotted the cluster of maple and oak trees. There were impressions in the tall grass where someone had walked, a clear path to the cave. Following Henry's tracks, I broke into a run. "Henry!" I called as I reached the mouth of the cave.

His low response echoed from the interior. "Robin?"

"Yes, it's me," I answered, both relieved to hear his voice and nervous about facing him. I ducked down to enter the cave, and suddenly I could see nothing but a silvery blast of light. Henry was shining a flashlight on me.

"Thank goodness you're here, Robin!" he cried. "But how did you—I mean, I thought I'd be stuck in here forever."

He aimed his flashlight at his leg, and I saw that it was wedged between two stones. "I can't move it. I slipped and turned my ankle," he explained. "I think it's sprained."

"Oh, Henry, are you all right?" I clambered toward him, a rush of pity and tenderness overcoming me.

"Of course not, I'm stuck," he answered with irritation. It was obvious that he was in a great deal of pain. "I need someone big to get me out of here."

"Do you think your foot's broken?"

"I don't know. Once I'm out of here, we can find out." He groaned.

"Let me try to lift you." In spite of Henry's protests, I hooked my arms under his shoulders, but to no avail.

"I think we need two people, Robin." Henry winced and tried to smile.

"OK, I'll get help. What would you have done if I hadn't come along?"

"I'd have been here until summer, and my aunt would have regretted sending me to a foreign country."

"Do you need my sweater?" I started to take it off.

"No, thank you," he said, stopping short as pain shot through his leg, "but it's very gallant of you to offer."

I took his flashlight and scrambled out of the cave, pulling my sweater close against me in the damp cold. I couldn't remember how far down the mountain the farmhouses were, so I just kept to the trail and walked for what seemed like ages. Finally the inviting light of a farmhouse winked at me from a distance, and I stumbled across a pasture toward it through an eerie fog.

I knocked at the door. A face appeared, eyeing me suspiciously, and I realized how odd it must seem for a young girl to be wandering in the mountains alone in the evening. The man inside was middle-aged, with curly red hair and the distinctly weathered features of a farmer.

I had no French sentence formed when he answered the door, and I panicked momentarily. Meeting his questioning stare, I finally asked in his language, "Can you help me, please?" He didn't reply, but puffed on his pipe, waiting for more information. "There has been an accident in the cave," I explained. "My friend is badly hurt."

"Ah, *oui*." The man's facial expression altered abruptly. He grabbed a leather coat off a hook near the door, shouted to his wife that he would return later, and motioned for me to follow him. His son hurried after us, carrying a thick rope. The two Swiss farmers blazed the way to the cave.

I had made myself understood with only a few words on the spur of the moment, and it almost felt natural. I half ran in order to catch up with the two men.

The temperature had dropped by the time we reached the cave. Henry's teeth were chattering, and the son wrapped his sweater around his shoulders.

"You sound like a rattling skeleton," I said, teasing Henry.

"You choose the dumbest times to crack jokes, Robin."

"Just trying to keep up your spirits," I explained, forcing what I hoped was a cheerful smile.

The farmer examined Henry's injured leg and tried to move him.

Henry groaned. "It's going to hurt too much."

"Henry, do you want us to save you, or do you want to rot here? Because if you do, it would be my pleasure to let you." I tried to laugh, but inside I was terribly nervous.

The two men finally managed to lift Henry with only a little movement of his injured ankle. While I was helping dislodge the rocks, I accidentally brushed his foot. He gave a low moan. I shone the flashlight on the bruised ankle. "Poor Henry," I whispered, surveying the swollen purple-and-blue area.

"Save your sympathy for after we get home," Henry said. Then he asked the names of his rescuers, which were Jacques and Pierre Valliat. The father and son carried Henry back to their house, where they had a truck. We hoisted Henry into the truck bed, and I crawled in next to him for the ride into town. He surveyed me with curiosity.

"Comfortable?" I asked him.

"Hmm. Why did you come up here all by yourself?" he wanted to know. "I thought you were finished with me."

"Look, Henry, I talked to Mr. List on the phone. He was looking for you and thought you and I would be together." I paused, then went on. "He explained what really happened yesterday. I didn't realize before that you thought *I* stood *you* up." I was embarrassed having to admit how unfair I'd been.

His eyes held mine. "And now?"

"Now, I want to apologize for how I acted yesterday. I got mad when you weren't home. I thought you'd stood me up and that you didn't want me involved in your research anymore. I thought you would rather go with Mr. List so you could get extra friendly with him, and since we were always arguing—" I knew I was babbling, but I couldn't stop.

"You really believed all that? And it really bothered you?" He reached for my hand. "Robin, I thought you couldn't stand me. You must admit, from the beginning you haven't been exactly friendly to me. Talking to you is like trying to talk to a shark sometimes. I never know when you're going to bite."

"That's an awfully ugly way to look at me," I complained.

"But, Robin, I didn't understand what I'd done wrong. Then I finally figured out that you'd been the star of List's class before I came along, and then I got the teaching position that you wanted. After that, everything snowballed. I know if I were you I probably would've been less than friendly under those circumstances, too."

"Yeah, you're right about all that stuff, Henry," I admitted grudgingly. "But you were terrible to me, too. You were so cocky, I used to wonder why you thought you were so wonderful. I mean, I thought you were a pretty great guy, but you didn't have to rub it in all the time."

"Gee, Robin, I guess we both can dish it out, but neither of us can take it."

I smiled in agreement. "But you know," he continued, "about me acting like I thought I was so cool and everything—well, it's hard for me to say this, but it was all just a big front." He lowered his eyes. "I've always felt I had to excel, ever since I was a little kid, and I've always pushed myself and pretended I knew I was the best. When I saw how annoyed that got you, I couldn't help but rub it in more and give you a bad time. See, I wanted your attention. And also," he looked up mischievously, "you're so cute when you're mad. I'm sorry," he finished sincerely.

"I'm sorry, too. For being a shark." I suddenly understood what life must have been like for a lonely little kid with no folks. That had probably held Henry apart from other kids, so naturally he'd tried hard to get attention. And I'd been mean to him! I felt awful.

"When you avoided me at school today, I thought it was really over with you," Henry said. "So I came up here by myself."

"I'm so sorry, Henry."

Henry put his arm around my waist. "Mr. List

came over early to tell me about Monsieur Gerard, who thought he knew my family," he continued. "I was back for you early. I still haven't gone to see my cousins because I wanted you to go with me, the way we'd planned. It will be more fun." His arm tightened about my waist, and I snuggled closer. It felt good to be next to him, good to know he really did care. We sat silently. I could see pain etched across his handsome face.

"You know, Robin, I sat in the cave and tried to imagine what it was like when families stayed there until they were able to find homes. We'll come back here, too, when my foot's better."

"I'd love to," I said softly. I wasn't turning down any more of Henry's invitations.

"By the way, thanks for rescuing me." He grinned. "You managed to get help all by yourself speaking French? I'm impressed. Wow!" Then he leaned over and kissed me, holding me close. Our bodies warmed each other against the cool, damp night.

Chapter Twelve

Thérèse Bouchet answered the door with a toddler in her arms. "*Allô*, Henry!" She clasped Henry to her in a tight embrace, causing the baby to wail. Thérèse was a small, efficient-looking woman with spare features and hair the color of straw. The baby was chubby with a few dark wisps of hair and didn't resemble his mother one bit. Henry introduced me, and I received the same warm hug.

"Edouard! Edouard!" Thérèse called to her husband. She held up the baby's pudgy hand for us to shake. The child smiled broadly at Henry, showing off a few teeth.

Edouard sauntered out to meet us, and I was immediately struck by the family resemblance. He had the same green eyes as Henry, the same narrow nose and face, but he was a very large man, much larger than I imagined Henry would ever be.

After chatting about our trip, we were invited to a beautifully set table of white-and-blue china and cut flowers as a centerpiece. Lunch consisted of homemade soup and bread, cheese, fish, and vegetables.

Edouard Bouchet showed us gilt-framed photographs of his father, which hung above an ornate sideboard. "He looks a lot like my father," Henry said in French.

"My father, Maurice, is a family hero," Edouard told us, "because he went back to France and helped liberate Paris. The years before that, he was a Maquis, bringing refugees over the mountains into Switzerland. My mother and older brother, who is no longer alive, came here much earlier. My father joined them later."

"Why didn't he return to France?" I asked.

"France was a mess after the war. My mother had made new friends and was very content to stay in Switzerland. They both had seen enough of the war, so they stayed."

Looking at Henry's face, I could see how important family was to him. For years he'd been missing the closeness of a family. This meeting was helping to fill the void. Our eyes met across the table.

Henry inquired after Paulette, his other cousin, Edouard's sister.

"She's living in France, but she travels a great deal," Edouard explained. "Someday you must meet."

"Next trip," winked Thérèse, jiggling the child on her lap. "Let me put the baby down for his nap, and we'll get out our photo albums." The baby, also named Edouard, let out a protesting wail but was whisked firmly off to his crib. Edouard senior dug a stack of albums out of the sideboard and spread them on the floor, where Henry and I sat cross-legged and began poring over them.

There were yellowed photos of Maurice, a handsome man; Edouard and Thérèse as a young couple; baby Edouard and Paulette, who also looked a lot like Henry. In one photo her wavy hair blew loose in the breeze, and she had on her face that same curious look Henry often had.

It was late when we finally left the Bouchets. Henry and I walked arm in arm to the train station, talking about our visit. He filled me in on the gaps in conversation that I'd missed. "Edouard said he'd visited the cave, too. His father stayed there for a few days before finding a home of his own. Many Swiss people opened their homes to refugees during the war," he said. "I told Edouard and Thérèse how much you helped me with the research and about how you rescued me."

I smiled. It had been a week since Henry had hurt his foot in the cave. Since then he'd constantly been quick to remind me of my heroism. He'd spent a few days recovering while I brought him Swiss chocolates to gorge on, and now he was walking with only a slight limp.

Suddenly Henry drew me close. I ran my fingers through his tousled hair, pulling him nearer. I loved the feeling of his arms around me and his lips on mine. The long wail of the train whistle interrupted us, and we hurried to the edge of the platform. Henry's arm slid about my waist, and we boarded the train entwined in each other's arms.

Chapter Thirteen

Our three-week stay was, sadly, at a close. The next day we'd board the train that would take us to the airport. None of us liked to think of leaving our host families, whom we'd grown close to, yet we all reminded ourselves that our host "brothers and sisters" would be coming to the US soon for their own three-week stays. The school threw a goodbye party for all of us.

When I came in, Elise smiled mischievously. "There's someone I want you to meet," she said. She singled out a boy with reddish-brown hair, blue eyes, and an angular face. His arched eyebrows made him look just a little amused at the world.

"This is Jules," she announced happily.

"Hi," Jules greeted us, obviously pleased to know an English word.

"Hi," I said. Tracy and Melissa came over to introduce themselves, too. By the looks on Jules's and Elise's faces, we could tell that they were very fond of each other.

Dominique was there with René, whom we had discussed a great deal since she'd started seeing him. It was customary for groups of teens to go out together, so I'd gone with Dominique and René to movies and concerts, and I liked him. He was quiet where Dominique was vivacious, and she kept him constantly informed on things American.

He wore a "Save the Whales" T-shirt, and when I asked if he knew what it meant, he said that he didn't. "It's American," he said proudly, which made me giggle.

Henry and I danced beneath the decorations, little Swiss and American flags hanging across the ceiling. The table centerpiece was an artful combination of flags and flowers. There were also two cakes, one shaped like Switzerland and one like the US. Tracy, Melissa, and Dominique joked about wanting to eat certain cantons or states.

"Elise and Jules are cute together," Henry commented, watching them dance close. "They go together like you and I do."

"Except they never seem to have any trouble the way we did."

"We were both a little difficult at times," Henry admitted.

"I think I might understand you now, Henry," I told him softly.

He kissed my forehead lightly, brushing a few stray hairs out of the way with his lips. "Did I tease you too much? Don't you know that that was the exact measure of how much I liked you?"

"Wow, Henry, you really were difficult," I said, recalling how terrible he had been to me.

"I thought you didn't like me. You were constantly pushing me away," he reminded me.

"I was. You scared me."

"You scared me, too. I got defensive. One part of me wanted to keep you at an arm's length while the other part couldn't stay away from you."

"Is that the part that invited me to go to the library with you?" I gazed into his deep eyes, thinking about how much I wished the trip didn't have to end. I'd treasured every moment, and especially the time spent with Henry.

"Yes. That's also the part that got awfully upset when I thought you didn't want to go. Also when you didn't wait the first time we were supposed to go to Lausanne."

"I didn't make things any easier," I whispered.

"No, you didn't. But the best things in life aren't always easy." He gazed at me fondly.

The memory of the bon voyage party at Ellen's house back home came to me. That had been only three weeks earlier, but so much had happened since. If someone had told me then I would ever be floating happily in Henry Bouchet's arms, I would have told him he was crazy!

But now, I realized, I was nervous about staying in Henry's arms. For some reason I kept feeling that the moment we stepped onto US soil, the dream would end. I wanted to memorize every expression, every emotion, every scene we'd shared together. I thought about the first time Henry had kissed me, the time I'd noticed our reflections in the train window, how my heart had lurched at the sight of him hurt in the cave. I knew I'd never forget any of it. Besides, I'd taken four rolls of film, with Henry's help. We'd have pictures of the Bouchets, Sardeaus, and Aubers and all the incredible sites and monuments.

I looked up at Henry, touching his cheek with one finger as we danced. "I was just thinking that this trip has been such a dream, I don't want it to end," I told him.

"I know what you mean," he said, squeezing me tightly. "But someday we'll come back."

Mr. List had warned us that we would feel very sad about leaving our host families, but nothing could prepare us for how we felt as we left for the airport. I had grown fond of two families, not just one.

I took flowers to the Sardeaus before leaving. I was so emotional that all I could do was present the flowers to the family, saying in French, "For you. Thank you." Although my French was vastly improved and I felt a hundred percent more confident with the language, feelings were still difficult for me to express.

Since Madame Auber had received so many bouquets because of her broken arm, instead of flowers I gave her family some molded maple sugar candy that I'd brought for them from home. Dominique and I cried during our farewell embrace. We had grown so close during my stay. The only thing that made parting less painful was the thought of her upcoming visit to my house.

"You'd think when you can't communicate perfectly with people, it would be a relief to leave," Henry commented. "But it isn't at all."

"It reminds me of leaving camp. After a whole summer, you almost become a family."

Henry lifted my suitcase to carry it to the train. "Hey, what do you have in this suitcase, bricks?"

"No, but I have every right to carry bricks on board if I want to," I told him.

He rolled his eyes. "Oh, no, here we go again."

I laughed and followed him, smoothing the front of my new, loose-fitting violet sweater. I'd bought pumps to match so that I really looked European.

"That outfit looks good on you," Henry said, standing back in the aisle to get a better look.

"Thank you." I grinned. And now I was sure that Henry wasn't being sarcastic at all.

On the way to the airport, I took more pictures, remembering how startlingly different the countryside had looked to me when we first arrived. Now it was familiar, but it would always fill me with awe.

I thought of how much I'd miss traveling with Henry. I hoped he wouldn't forget what we'd shared on this trip. It would be so easy to go home and slip into the old routine, losing the romance of Switzerland in daily life.

When we boarded the plane, Henry grinned at me. "You're not going to complain about sitting with me this time, are you?"

"No." I laughed. "This time I know I'm in great company."

"At least I'm not a salesman trying to sell you a life insurance policy," he said.

As we sat down, I noticed Tracy waving her arms at me from the back of the plane.

"Be back in a minute," I told Henry.

"It looks like you and Henry are getting pretty tight," Melissa said, from her seat next to Tracy. "He's crazy about you."

"It all worked out, didn't it?" Tracy exclaimed enthusiastically. "Remember how we all joked about having a Swiss romance?"

"One out of three isn't bad," Melissa added. "And we might've guessed it would be you, Robin."

"Your friends approve of us?" Henry quipped when I returned to my seat.

"Yes. We've become a hot subject," I told him.

He studied me thoughtfully for a moment, then took my hand and stroked each finger. "You know, I don't want to go home and lose what we've had together. And I don't want this to be the last trip we ever take. I can't tell you how much I like you. Let's plan to travel together when we get home, OK? Maybe we can go to Maine or Vermont. A trip like that won't be as far, but it'll be just as much fun."

"That sounds fantastic," I replied, my fears

put to rest. He'd been feeling the same way I had. And to think, three weeks before, I'd thought Henry Bouchet was the most impossible guy in the whole world.

We hope you enjoyed reading this book. All the titles currently available in the Sweet Dreams series are listed on the next two pages. They are all available at your local bookshop or newsagent, though should you find any difficulty in obtaining the books you would like, you can order direct from the publisher, at the address below. Also, if you would like to know more about the series, or would simply like to tell us what you think of the series, write to:

Kim Prior,
Sweet Dreams,
Transworld Publishers Limited,
61−63 Uxbridge Road,
Ealing, London W5 5SA.

To order books, please list the title(s) you would like, and send together with your name and address, and a cheque or postal order made payable to TRANSWORLD PUBLISHERS LIMITED. Please allow cost of book(s) plus 20p for the first book and 10p for each additional book for postage and packing.

(The above applies to readers in the UK and Ireland only.)

If you live in Australia or New Zealand, and would like more information about the series, please write to:

Sally Porter,
Sweet Dreams
Corgi & Bantam Books,
26 Harley Crescent,
Condell Park,
N.S.W. 2200,
Australia.

Kiri Martin
Sweet Dreams
c/o Corgi & Bantam Books
New Zealand,
Cnr. Moselle and Waipareira
Avenues,
Henderson,
Auckland,
New Zealand.

Dear *SWEET DREAMS* reader,

Since we started publishing SWEET DREAMS almost two years ago, we have received hundreds of letters telling us how much you like the series and asking for details about the books and the authors.

We are getting to know quite a lot about our readers by now and we think that many of you would like a club of your own. That's why we're setting up THE SWEET DREAMS CLUB.

If you would like to become a member, just fill in the details below and send it to me together with a cheque or postal order for £1.50 (payable to The Sweet Dreams Club) to cover the cost of our postage and administration. Your membership package will contain a special SWEET DREAMS membership card, and a SWEET DREAMER newsletter packed full of information about the books and authors, beauty tips, a fascinating quiz and lots more besides (including a fabulous special offer!).

Now fill in the coupon (in block capitals please), and send, with payment, to:

The Sweet Dreams Club,
Freepost (PAM 2876),
London W5 5BR.

N.B. No stamp required.

I would like to join The Sweet Dreams Club.

Name:...

Address:..

....

I enclose a cheque/postal order for £1.50, made payable to The Sweet Dreams Club.

This offer applies to the UK and Ireland only.